Guardian's Nightmare

Darren Simon

DIVERTIR
PUBLISHING
Salem, NH

Guardian's Nightmare

Darren Simon

On the Cover:
Laura Jamison (Photo by Eric Jamison)

Cover photos :

Pegasus
(http://www.bigstockphoto.com/image-16509749/stock-photo-pegasus)

Golden Gate Bridge at Night
(http://www.bigstockphoto.com/image-549428/stock-photo-golden-gate-bridge)

Medallion (back cover) by Kenneth Tupper

Cover design by Kenneth Tupper

Published by Divertir Publishing LLC
PO Box 232
North Salem, NH 03073
http://www.divertirpublishing.com/

ISBN-13: 978-1-938888-06-9
ISBN-10: 1-938888-06-5

Library of Congress Control Number: 2014938974

Printed in the United States of America

Dedication

This book is dedicated to my loving wife and two sons whose support and inspiration keep me motivated and to my parents who taught me to love reading and encouraged me to show my imagination through writing.

Contents

Chapter 1

A Far Away World

The Guardian rode hard and fast, his wind-horse charging through the Valley of Columns where towering trees—their trunks spiraling toward the emerald sky—seemed to keep the heavens aloft. The wild grass underfoot glowed as twilight beckoned and the few lingering rays of gold touched the clouds.

At the Valley's edge, fires from the enemy camp cast an orange haze against the oncoming dusk. Beneath the dancing afterglow of the rising flames stood an army more than twice the size of his own.

Tugging on the reins, the Guardian ordered the steed to slow its airborne gallop. The mighty horse, which raced three feet above the ground, touched land, and slowed to a trot before stopping. The Guardian's two top generals, also atop wind-horses, were soon at his side.

"I must continue the rest of the way on my own," the Guardian declared.

"My lord, forgive me, but I cannot allow that." General Tribon's red beard blew in a gentle wind.

"I agree with Tribon." The younger General Ibala frowned. "This meeting is ill advised and allowing you to carry on by yourself is most dangerous."

The Guardian smiled and nodded first to Tribon, a giant man and one of the Guardian's oldest friends, and then to the young but wise Ibala. "Rest assured, I understand your concern and appreciate your loyalty. If I do not return, I need to know that the knights of the Ten Unified Kingdoms will have you to guide them. I am depending on you both."

"Yes, my lord," the generals lamented.

"Goodbye and ride well." The Guardian offered his hand in a final gesture. "Let the morning bring great fortune upon us all."

His generals' lowered eyes foretold the same doom he felt. Even the greatest warriors from the early days couldn't withstand such a massive gathering of evil. Despite that, they would fight hard and lead well should he not survive the night. Maybe with faith they would be victorious.

With one last nod, the Guardian turned and clicked his horse with his boots to forge on alone. He rode until he neared the army of Horeng and halted just for a moment to take in its grand scale. It was an army tens of thousands strong. Torches burned blood red, pouring black smoke into the darkening skies. War banners covered the land.

The stench of rotting flesh filled the air. The Guardian covered his nose with a gloved hand. By now he was familiar with the foul odor emanating from this army of mindless half-man half-wolf beasts. Forged by sorceress Theodora to serve her dark will, the Horeng stunk of the death they caused throughout the Unified Kingdoms.

With a pat to his wind-horse's neck, his trusted companion slowly trotted forward until they crossed through the Horeng's front lines. A chorus of snarls and howls sounded in a chain reaction. The Guardian assumed it must be some form of communication through the lines informing all that he was there and that he was to be watched closely. Their yellow eyes bore down on him.

Two Horeng dressed in black armor and long snout-covering helmets rode from the shadows on horses draped in covering as dark as midnight. Without speaking, the two Horeng turned and rode deeper into the encampment along a trail of crackling torches. The Guardian understood that he was meant to follow.

He sensed archers nearby, their arrows aimed at him. He couldn't see them, but they were there. The archers' claws eerily scraped together as they held their bow strings taut.

Finally, his escorts reached Theodora's tent where two more Horeng stood guard. Growls rose from their throats. The Guardian gazed at them as he climbed from his steed then patted the animal on the neck one more time. He approached the two sentries with his right hand deceptively loose on the handle of his sword. From that position, he could destroy them before they had a chance to blink.

"Let him pass." The two guards stepped aside with snarls of frustration at the command from inside the tent. The Guardian tipped his head slightly to the two sentries then crossed through the entrance.

He entered a lavishly decorated chamber—not a makeshift shelter on the front line of a war. A floating collage of twisted golden, silver, and bronze crowns danced in a corner, forming a warped piece of art. They belonged to the fallen kings and queens he had failed to protect. They belonged to those who had been his friends.

2

A second floating display, the broken swords of generals struck down in battle, swirled in another corner. Dried blood covered some of the steel. The blades danced as if the spirits of those great leaders still wielded the weapons.

The furniture inside the tent—a table, bed and throne—was made from human bones. Skulls lined the base of the bed and held torches illuminating the tent at each corner.

Closing his eyes, he fought off the sickness building in his stomach. Was this real, or just an elaborate magic creation for his benefit? The Guardian steeled himself. "Theodora, show yourself."

"I am right here." Dressed in a dark robe with a cape trailing behind it, Theodora appeared next to the floating crowns. With the back of her right hand, she tenderly stroked one of them. "I saw you admiring my artwork. Do you like it? I find art so comforting in these times of war."

The Guardian's hands formed fists. *I should strike her down.* He knew such an action would not succeed. Theodora was much too powerful to fall that easily.

"Go ahead," she challenged.

"What?"

"Unsheathe your sword and kill me. You know that is what you want to do."

"That is not why I am here." The Guardian stepped farther into the tent but kept a sword-blade's distance from Theodora. His face burned red and his heart raced. *Remain calm. She wishes to bait you.*

"Well then, Michala, my dear brother-in-law, it is so very pleasing to see you again." The words slithered across her lips as she smiled and bowed.

Michala did not respond immediately. He glared at her, studying her appearance. He had seen her before. Still, his wife's younger sister appeared so different every time their paths crossed, as if she were aging years with each passing day. No one would ever guess she was Queen Assara's younger sibling.

Thin hair hugged the contours of an ashen gray face, with eyes like dead orbs streaked by crimson lines. Once as beautiful as Assara, she had stopped being human and had become something else after turning to the dark arts.

"Theodora, what have you become? You gave up your soul out of jealousy for your sister's crown. You had so much potential as a leader. You could have ruled at your sister's side as First Princess of Latara."

Theodora's eyes glowed red. "You know I was the one fit to serve as queen, brother-in-law. I was the strong one. I was the wisest. I was born to lead. But because of some aging, misguided tradition, my sister was named

3

queen simply for being born first. It was time for a change, and I have brought such change. And the world, my world, will be a better place for all."

"For all! You mean for you. Why, Theodora? Why did you have to destroy so many lives? You already had powerful magic. Why did you have to feed on all the other conjurers?" The Guardian sighed. "I regret my failure to protect all those men, women, and children—all those magical creatures. You took their lives and enslaved the non-magics, all for your own twisted hunger for power, and I couldn't stop you. What is sad, sister-in-law, is that you don't even know you're just a pawn—a vessel for the dark magic. It uses you more than you use it."

Theodora clasped her hands and placed them against her chin. "Those who gave their spirits to me should be honored to have done so, for I am Empress. And soon your meek army shall fall for the last time. I have destroyed all of the Unified Kingdoms but my sister's—all but Latara. Tomorrow it shall fall as well. Then all non-magics will serve me, and I shall find all conjurers among your people and unify their magic within me."

The Guardian took a deep breath. "Why is it you sent for me tonight?"

Theodora's eyes softened. "Michala, we could stop all this foolishness right now if you would just return what is rightfully mine. Return the medallion you have stolen from me and I will end my campaign. There will be no more death, no more destruction. There will be peace."

"Theodora, I don't know what you're talking about. I have taken nothing from you."

"Liar! I don't know how you managed it, but you found a way to steal my medallion and I want it back. Return it, and I will spare my sister's land. Refuse and you, my sister, your child and all who call Latara home will perish at daybreak."

The Guardian approached Theodora and grasped her robe with both hands. "You cannot touch my child; not now, not ever. And as for this medallion you speak of, I do not possess it, so take your threats to someone who fears you. I do not."

Theodora slapped him across the face. "You fool! Do you know what you have done?"

"Made you mortal," Michala said. He released Theodora's robes.

"No, brother-in-law, you have passed a death sentence on your people and on your Queen, your wife, the woman you have vowed to protect. And do not think your child will escape me. I will search all eternity—I will never cease until the child of my sister dies."

4

"That's the point, sister-in-law. Without the medallion, you no longer have all eternity."

Theodora shrieked. Her body shook as she paced, her fingers clawing at her face. Then she calmed. "With a simple wave of my hand I could end your life now!"

"Do as you will."

"No, I will let you live so that you can see your army destroyed and see your precious Latara crumble."

Her words pierced him, but he buried his feelings. Instead, the Guardian turned from Theodora in silence, left her tent, and then found his wind-horse outside. Without hesitation, he jumped onto his steed then called out, "Yaaa!"

The wind-horse sprinted through the Horeng camp, passing along the path outlined by the torches. When they reached the front line, the Guardian drew his sword then slashed at a wooden post that held aloft a war banner. He didn't stop to see it fall. It was a meaningless gesture, but he smiled anyway as the Horeng howled their protests.

Bolting away from the enemy, the Guardian half expected Theodora's monsters to pursue him, but glancing back the land behind him was still. Once far enough away, the Guardian called out, "Hold on, boy." The horse slowed and then stopped.

The castle of Latara stood in the distance where he knew Queen Assara, his wife, watched for his return and kept vigil over her people from the castle's observation deck. Three golden moons, the Tri-Queens of the Night, climbed high above the castle.

Tomorrow at sunrise the battle would begin. He was ready and would use his power as a Guardian to surprise Theodora and perhaps bring about a quick victory. He was, after all, a warrior. A warrior always had to have faith. But his meager forces were tired. They were brave and they would fight hard, but without help, they couldn't do much more on the battlefield.

If only he had convinced the Dragon Lord to join in the war to stop Theodora. If only...

The Guardian brushed off that thought. At least she was weakened by the loss of the medallion. Theodora was right. He had taken it from her. Perhaps in the right hands it could be used to defeat the sorceress, but the medallion was pure evil. Contact with it twisted the mind, and since it could not be destroyed by conventional weapons or magic, he hid the medallion where she might never be able to reach it.

Images of his baby girl, Aneera, filled his mind from her sandy blonde hair to her light blue eyes. She was safe for now. He had used his abilities to open a gateway and send her to a new world, assigning his most trusted friend to protect the child. Still, Theodora's words were more than just a threat.

The sorceress would seek out his daughter in the hunt for her medallion and one day Theodora might discover a way to reach that world.

If she did, not only would Theodora possibly find the girl, but the medallion as well, for he had chosen to hide both in that world he had come to know as Earth.

Chapter 2

On Earth, Present Day

"What I wouldn't give to be a superhero." Charlee gazed up from her favorite comic book. She liked reading about heroes—people who stood up for what was right and weren't afraid of anything or anybody, especially bullies like Tina Lomeli. Tina made life a nightmare for all middle-school aged boys and girls at Myron T. Applebee Middle School who didn't meet her stuck-up standards. Any girl who read comic books was sure to end up on Tina's nerd list.

Charlee set the comic book on her bed. Looking at the superhero posters covering the far wall, she recognized none of the qualities that made them so heroic in herself. No matter how badly she wanted to be like them, being thirteen years old and scared of pretty much everything tended to rule out any chances of becoming a hero.

She laughed at the rainbow shaped nightlight on her dresser as she nibbled on the ends of her hair. "What kind of hero still needs a nightlight after watching a scary movie or sulks when her family moves to San Francisco, leaving behind the farm town with all her friends? Heroes don't cry just because making friends at a new school isn't going well. Geez! Some superheroes crossed the universe to make their home on Earth. They never cried about it."

Charlee caught her image in the mirror on the closet door. "I can't be a hero. What comic book hero is chubby, has long stringy hair, a freckled face and green-framed glasses with thick, Coke-bottle lenses? None!" She swallowed a lungful of air and blew away a strand of brown hair from her cheek. "I'm not even the slightest bit cool."

The kids at school reminded her of this often—led by that creep, Tina. One day in particular, Tina, joined by a group of kids from the wealthier neighborhoods of San Francisco's Central District, cornered Charlee at her locker and unleashed a flurry of insults.

"Where you going, Chub…I mean Charlee?" Tina tossed her long auburn hair from her perfect complexion. A heavy layer of makeup covered her cheeks. Dark eyeliner accentuated icy blue eyes. They were cruel eyes, filled with venom.

"Just to lunch," Charlee answered, peering up at Tina, who stood a foot taller.

"Maybe you should skip a lunch or two." Tina sneered, gesturing toward Charlee's rounded stomach. Tina peered into Charlee's open locker. A comic book rested atop a math book. Tina grabbed it. "You read comic books? What a loser."

Charlee snatched the comic book and tried to sound tough. "Oh yeah, ever hear of Comic Con in San Diego? Are the tens of thousands who attend losers too? I don't think so."

"Whatever, nerd," Tina responded.

"Hey, why'd your parents name you Charlee?" asked Casey, a boy who served as Tina's main henchman.

"That's not her real name," said April, every bit the bully as Tina.

"Yeah, her real name is Charleya," quipped April's best friend, Ashley.

"And your last name is Smelton?" Casey asked. "Man, I'd hate to be you."

"Wait. Let's call her Smelly." April smiled, revealing ridiculously white teeth.

"Yeah! Smelly Smelton," chimed in Ashley, dressed in the same skirt, blouse, and pink heels as April.

"That's weak." Casey snorted with laughter. With that, the verbal assault ended. With one last glare down at Charlee, Tina joined the others, strolling away as if Charlee wasn't even there. As if she didn't matter.

A superhero wouldn't let them get away with their games. A superhero would stand up for herself. She spotted her plus-sized jeans lying on her bedroom floor. "Yeah, I'm definitely not a hero."

The familiar rumble of her dad's car interrupted Charlee's thoughts. The yellow Skylark, dubbed the "monster," noisily pulled up the driveway and into the garage. Her dad, Professor Smelton, climbed the steps into the main hallway that led to the kitchen of their two-story Victorian home.

"Charlee, will you come down here please? I've got a surprise for you, and I think you're going to like it."

She ignored him.

"Hurry down. I think this is just the ticket to lift your spirits."

Rolling her eyes, she opened the door to her room and slowly trudged downstairs.

"There you are, honey. Come on." Her dad grinned at the base of the stairs as he rubbed his well-trimmed black beard. His dark eyes beamed through round wire-framed glasses.

Charlee glanced at her mom, who offered a stern nod. Even her two-year-old sister, Megan, nestled in their mom's arms, offered a harsh expression as if to say, *"Deal with it, big sis."*

"Follow me." Her dad dashed into the garage. Charlee slunk like a zombie after him, glaring at the man who had ripped her away from her old life to accept some San Francisco State teaching job.

Once in the garage, her dad loosened his tie, slipped to the rear of the Skylark and opened the trunk. He grunted and huffed while removing an object from inside. Charlee perked up and rubbed her hands. Maybe he had got her something really cool—a new computer—her own TV.

"Come see," her dad breathed heavily.

Cautious, Charlee slid around the side of the car until she reached the trunk then spied the gift. She blinked once, twice, three times at what must be the ugliest bike…ever.

"What do you think, Charlee? She's a beauty, right?" Her dad lifted up the rear garage door that led to the backyard, exposing the bike to the last bit of soft late afternoon sunshine. "Here, now you can see it in better light." He pushed the bike into the backyard.

Charlee stared glumly at the bike then at her dad and once more at the bike. "What is it?"

"Well, honey, I know you've been feeling a bit down, and since we ran over your other bike with the moving van you need a new one. I was hoping this might cheer you up." He rested his hands on her shoulders. "In case I haven't said it lately, Charlee, you mean the world to me."

Wow! Did he really think a lame bike was going to make everything all right? She turned to the bike. It had to be a reject from the Sixties. Rust and scratches covered the white-painted frame and chrome handlebars. The banana-shaped seat and white-walled tires aged it even more. To top it off, the bike had one of those upside-down U-shaped chrome backrests. She strolled once around the bike, studying it. It was truly the ugliest heap of scrap metal ever.

Maybe if it was a cool mountain bike or a beach cruiser, Charlee might consider riding it. But this…this was a used, old-fashioned, faded white junk heap that should have been put out of its misery a long time ago.

"I just couldn't help myself." Her dad smiled wide. "I was walking through the campus today as part of my afternoon exercise and there it was leaning up against a tree with a sign on the handlebars that said, 'Free Bike. Please Give It A Good Home.' I couldn't resist it."

He stopped to catch his breath, a childlike glee shining in his eyes. "It's like a bike I had when I was your age. You know the one. I have a picture of it in my den. Do you like it? I mean, I know it's not much to look at right now, but I thought we could spend some time fixing it up—just you and me. It will be fun."

"I don't want it," she said coldly then stormed from the garage back upstairs to her room. She slammed the door and rushed to the window. Her dad still stood in the backyard by the bike, his eyes downcast.

Charlee's jaw tightened. She had hurt him. Why shouldn't she? He hurt her by moving to San Francisco. Voices below caught her attention. Charlee's mom gently hugged her husband and gave him a soft kiss on the cheek.

Sliding her window open an inch, Charlee listened to the conversation below.

"I guess this was a mistake," her dad sighed.

"No. Charlee is going through an adjustment right now." Her mom placed a hand on his shoulder. "I'm sure she likes the bike. She's just not ready to show it yet."

"I'm not talking about the bike. Maybe moving to the city was a mistake. What was I thinking, taking her away from all her friends? What kind of a father am I?"

A lousy one. Charlee shook her head in silent protest.

"Dear, you're the best. You want the best for us and you are a protector." Her mom's eyes widened. "That's why you took the teaching position. That's why you brought us here. You're a loving father and you have always been the guardian of this family."

Charlee raised an eyebrow. What did she mean, protector…guardian?

"I'm not so sure." Her dad bowed his head.

"Well, I am. Now go inside and wash your hands for dinner."

Her mom and dad held each other tight for a moment more. Then they walked hand in hand to the garage and back into the house. Soon, there was a hard knock at Charlee's door. Without waiting for an invitation, her mom swung open the door and marched inside, her expression angry. "What was that down there? Your father did a nice thing for you and you were just rude."

"Sorry, Mom, but I don't want that stupid bike." Charlee looked away from her mom. "Why'd he have to get it for me, anyway?"

"Look at me, Charlee Smelton." Her mom brushed away long sandy blonde bangs from her forehead, revealing light blue eyes. Charlee wished she had her mom's eyes instead of the brown orbs that made her look more like her dad. "I am surprised at you. He brought it for you because he loves you very much."

10

"But, Mom, you saw the bike. It's a reject."

"You know how your father loves classics. Just look at his car. You know he means well." Her mom sighed. The frown lines in her face seemed deeper. "Right now, your father is downstairs feeling rejected. I don't think it's fair to make him feel that way."

"But—"

"Honey, I know you're having a rough time. But you are stronger than you think. Remember that."

Charlee shrugged. She tried to convey a lot in that gesture. She hoped her mom understood.

"Tell you what. After dinner, let's have a conversation—you, me and your father—about school. Let's see if we can figure some things out together. Right now, put the bike in the garage, wash your hands, and set the table for dinner. And apologize to your father." Her mom didn't wait for a response. She turned and walked out of the room. Sulking, Charlee followed her to the stairs and lumbered down the steps into the garage and out to the backyard where the bike was waiting.

Beads of sweat formed on her forehead as she examined the two-wheeled white nightmare. "You're the ugliest hunk of junk I've ever seen. Do you know how much trouble I'd be in if others saw me riding you? That will never happen. I just want to get that straight right now."

She swiftly kicked at the right front tire but missed and tumbled to the ground. It wasn't really that she missed…the tire just seemed to move out of the way. She sat on the hard cement, glaring at the bike.

Charlee laughed at herself and stood up to push the bike into the garage. When her hands touched the bars, energy shot through her body. It was like when she accidentally touched an exposed wire on an old lamp but worse. Her whole body tingled. She trembled uncontrollably and dropped to her knees.

"What the…?"

As the tingling faded, Charlee stood and ran her fingers through her hair, which crackled from static cling. Something was very wrong. She had to get away from the bike as quickly as possible. Charlee dashed into the garage, up the steps and into the house. She rushed by her mom, hoping to avoid any questions.

No such luck. "Charlee, did you put the bike in the garage?"

"Uh, not yet, Mom. Not yet." She sprinted upstairs and back into her room, slamming the door shut. She went to the window and stared down at the bike. *Strange! Very strange!*

Chapter 3

Is It A Dream?

One minute, Charlee slept safely buried under the covers. The next minute, she stood alone on a narrow grassy path lined on either side by thick trees. Branches far above her head arched, forming a thick canopy and shrouding her in shadows. Streaks of sunlight dotted the ground, but not enough to ease the chill she felt climbing up her back.

A breeze whistled as it blew along the pathway and rustled her hair. Charlee dropped to her knees as the sensation of fingers grazing her shoulder came from behind. No one was there. She scanned the ceiling of tree branches high above as the breeze brushed against her cheek. Were the branches reaching for her? Were the trees on either side of the path closing on her? Cold compressed her chest and made breathing difficult, or maybe it was the panic dancing around her stomach that allowed her only shallow breaths.

"I have to get out of here." She started walking gently down the path, which reminded her of the time she and her family toured an old gold mine on a vacation. She thought she could be brave and enter the dimly lit manmade cave, but once inside she cried until her parents returned her to the daylight. She didn't like closed in spaces, but this felt worse.

A gray haze covered the path ahead like an impenetrable barrier. Charlee stopped as a paralyzing fear gripped her. She wasn't alone. Any moment something would leap from the shadows to snatch her. Tears formed and slid down her cheeks. "Wait, this is just a dream. This isn't real. Why should I be scared?" She sniffed back the tears. "This may be a dream," she reminded herself, "but I've never had a dream feel this real before."

She eyed her gloomy surroundings one more time. The trees that lined the path blocked any view of what might lie beyond the green cavern. The little light trickling through the trees created shadowy dancing apparitions. While it was only the silhouette of the trees, she still trembled. Charlee quieted her breathing and stood still, listening for any peculiar noises. Sloshing water signaled a creek or lake nearby—but where? The gurgling bounced off the trees and surrounded her.

Something didn't feel right. "I don't want to be here."

Instinctively, she tried to adjust her glasses, but the thick spectacles were missing. *Strange.* A scratchy brown cloth shirt two sizes too big, with no buttons or collar, replaced the Superman T-shirt she had worn to bed.

"What's going on?" Heavy brown pants made of the same material as the shirt covered her legs instead of pajama bottoms. "Yes, I must be dreaming." On her feet, brown boots rose to her knees and around her waist wrapped tightly in some kind of animal skin hung a sword from a thick black belt.

Charlee gazed at the sword's handle. It was a simple T-shaped handle made of tarnished, aging metal, maybe silver.

A whisper plucked her attention. The sound grew until hundreds, maybe thousands, of faint murmurs echoed around her like a great wind rustling the leaves. But the breeze had disappeared and the leaves were still. Charlee covered her ears. "Please, stop!"

Giggling followed the whispers. Charlee spun around. Tiny unseen creatures—too many to count—seemed to laugh. "Who is that? Show yourself. Stop laughing. Please!"

"It is We." The words were deafening as a multitude of voices spoke at once.

Charlee stiffened. "Who said that?"

"Did We not just answer you?"

"Where are you?"

"We is right above you. Is that not obvious?"

Charlee peered at a low-hanging branch just over her head. The voices were loudest there. Standing on tiptoes, she slowly pulled it down to eye level.

A deep purple shade bathed each star-shaped leaf. They pulsated and generated warmth, as if they had a heartbeat. Charlee reached for one and slid her fingers over it. The leaf shivered and she quickly recoiled. "Weird! It feels like skin." She studied it closer. Its color shifted with each *heartbeat* from lavender to dark purple. They seemed alive.

"Please be careful in how you handle We."

"This can't be happening." Charlee released her grip on the branch and backed away.

"What do you mean?" the voices asked.

"Am I talking to a leaf?"

"No, you are talking to We. You are talking to all the leaves of the Our."

"What is the Our?" Charlee listened to her own words. She no longer spoke English. The words fashioned into a strange language—their language consisting of high-pitched vowel sounds strung together without any evident structure…yet they had meaning. How was she doing this?

"The Our is our tree," the voices explained. "That should be obvious to an intelligent being."

"I'm sorry. I've never spoken to leaves before. Can you tell me where I am?"

"You are home."

"I don't understand. What—"

Before she finished, a leaf broke free from the branch she had held and slowly floated to the ground.

"Oh, no! I'm sorry. If I hadn't tugged at the branch—"

"Do not grieve. When the lifecycle of one of We ends, We nourish Her. Then We will always be reborn for another cycle."

What a dream this is. Charlee started to speak again, but stopped when her breath formed a mist. A deeper chill settled over the tree-lined path. She wrapped her arms around her body. "I have to go now, We." She searched for a way home, perhaps a doorway. Nothing. Then a new sound drifted along the path. Singing! While sweet, the voice, perhaps a woman's, seemed sad and lonely. Hypnotized by the melody, Charlee momentarily ignored the cold, but the chattering of her teeth reminded her of the path's icy embrace. She rubbed her arms but continued to listen. "We, do you hear that singing?"

The leaf creatures did not respond.

Why?

Carefully, Charlee snuck along the pathway in the direction where the singing seemed the loudest. With one hand resting on the sword's handle, she broke into a sprint all the while peering for any openings in the trees. There! Panting, she slid to a stop when she came upon a side path, a tunnel cut into the trees illuminated by light that spilled in, possibly from the other end of this new trail.

As her breaths slowed, Charlee inched forward, hands out in front to push away low-hanging branches. She moved as quietly as possible over the leaves strewn across the trail. Every time she crushed a leaf, she stopped and silently cursed herself fearing she hurt the leaf creatures, whatever they were. Each step Charlee took brought her closer to a light source that shed warmth and broke through the murky forest.

With each step, the light intensified—almost painfully—and she had to shield her eyes. "Please be sunlight," she mouthed. "I'm tired of these shadows." A few steps farther and Charlee reached a clearing in the trees. Sunlight bathed her, chasing away the chill but the little hairs on her neck still stood at attention.

Blinking and rubbing her eyes, a creek came into focus flowing from the base of a small, lime-green hillock. The water glimmered and changed shades under the sunlight. It looked like the grape, orange and strawberry sodas Charlee liked so much. The creek defied gravity, flowing up and down the small hill as if pumps moved the water in both directions.

The singing continued. But where was the woman? Charlee shaded her eyes and surveyed the water. "Come on, where are you? Oh, there you are!" Downstream—or maybe upstream—the woman floated in the creek. Charlee crouched to remain hidden but didn't dare step back into the tunnel of greenery. She rubbed her eyes again. The woman was more like a ghost than flesh and blood. Draped in a flowing white dress, she drifted on her back in the water. Golden hair gleamed in the sunlight.

A rustling of leaves from the darkened path behind Charlee jolted her. She froze. *Remember, this is just a dream. Don't be scared.* She turned toward the sound and the silhouette of a man—a huge man—a giant man, faced her.

"Ahhh!" Charlee stumbled. She squeezed her eyes closed. "Please, giant, don't be there," she mumbled. "Please, I just want to be home, back in my bed."

But when she opened her eyes, the dream remained. She lay on the ground, and the huge figure knelt over her. Charlee studied the man. A cloak obscured his face, but a bushy beard, like a lion's mane, protruded from the cloak's hood. With each breath, the giant huffed like a bull ready to attack.

Charlee cleared her throat. "Uh…hi. I'm Charlee. Pl…please don't kill me. I'm just a kid."

"Quiet," the giant man commanded in a hushed, threatening voice. He rose to his full height, turned away, and then lumbered toward the woman in the creek.

He was going to kill the woman. She couldn't let that happen. But what could she do against a giant? She could think of only one course of action.

"Look out!" Charlee shouted.

§ § §

"Sweetheart, wake up." The soothing voice flowed through darkness, carried from a distance by the wind.

Charlee opened her eyes and blinked several times. Her heart hammered in her chest and she took fast, shallow breaths. She awoke, seeing her mom sitting beside her on the bed. "Mom?"

"You were having a bad dream."

"A dream! But it was so real," Charlee's heartbeat slowed.

Gently, her mom slid damp strands of hair off her forehead, blowing cool breaths of air over Charlee's skin. "That must have been some dream. You're covered in sweat. Well, whatever it was, you're safe now. Your father and I are in the next room."

"Thanks, Mom."

"Get some sleep now. We'll talk about your dream in the morning."

"Mom?"

"Yes."

"Why did he have to get me that stupid bike? If I ride it, everyone will make fun of me."

"Honey, you know your father means well. You've been sad since the move and he just wants to help."

"If he cared he wouldn't have made me leave my friends." Her mom sighed. Charlee knew why.

Her mom was at a loss for words because it had all been said. *Charlee, your father loves you. He's trying to make a good life for his family. He wasn't trying to hurt you by moving to the city. In time, this place will become home.* No matter how many times her mom uttered those words, Charlee still didn't believe them.

"I'm not going to ride that bike," Charlee blurted. "He can just forget that."

"Maybe you should give it a chance."

"Never."

Her mom moved to the bedroom door. "We'd both better get some sleep now. Tomorrow we will talk more." She left, closing the door behind her.

Charlee sat up in bed. In the glow of her nightlight, everything seemed safe. No one from the dream had followed her. *Of course I'm safe. It was just a dream.*

17

Chapter 4

Oh, Great...School

In the cafeteria of Myron Applebee, Charlee meandered through the lunch line and purchased a dry hamburger, cold fries, and a warm apple juice. Then she walked over to the same table—the same seat—she ate at every day all alone. Other social outcasts sat at the table, but even they kept their distance.

Charlee knew why. In Myron Applebee's pristine halls, Tina reigned as queen. If she targeted a student for her brand of bullying, others who had already faced similar humiliation stayed away. They feared being drawn back into the line of fire.

On this particular day, no one sat at the table. Charlee ate lunch completely alone until..."Hey, you mind if I sit here?"

Charlee glanced up to see Sandra Flores standing by the table, one hand holding a small paper bag, the other hand tucked into a pocket of her faded jeans. Long chestnut hair flowed around her face. When she smiled, Charlee noticed the braces on her teeth.

"Uh, no." Charlee slid over.

"Great. I wasn't sure if maybe you had this 'I'm-a-tough-girl-loner-so-back-off' thing working for you." Sandra sat and placed the crumpled bag on the table. She dove in and pulled out a foil-wrapped sandwich, banana, and a soda. Charlee fumbled with her own food.

Charlee knew Sandra from math class. Sandra was better at algebra than most students and wasn't afraid to argue with the teacher over an equation. She questioned the teacher at least once a class and didn't care when students rolled their eyes in frustration. If someone sighed, Sandra stared them down with her penetrating brown eyes. With a toss of her hair, she would then return to the teacher and continue with the challenge. *Why can't I be like that? Why is this tough girl sitting next to me?*

"Hey, why don't you take a picture? It lasts longer."

"What?" Charlee roused herself.

"You're staring at me. You know that's not polite."

Charlee looked away. "Sorry."

"Ah, I'm just kidding. You're Charlee, right?"

"Uh, yeah."

"Interesting name."

"It's really Charleya but I never liked that so somehow Charlee just stuck."

"Cool name either way," Sandra said. "You're kind of new here."

"This is my first year. We have math together." Charlee analyzed Sandra's smile. It seemed genuine. *Still,* Charlee thought, *she must be here to have a little fun at my expense.* Maybe Tina set it up as some trick.

"I'm Sandra. Good to meet you, Charlee."

"Uh, yeah. I mean, same here."

Silence followed. Her mouth drying, Charlee searched for something else to say. Sandra must have noticed. "Hey, if you want to be alone or something, just say the word, and I'll hit the road. That's cool. Sometimes I just want to be by myself, too."

"Uh, no," Charlee responded softly. "I'm sorry. I don't mean to be so lame or anything. It's just that no one ever asks to eat with me."

"I know the feeling." Sandra bit into her banana. "That's why I thought I'd come over here. You always eat alone and, well, I don't exactly have a bunch of friends crowding around me either. I was thinking maybe we could be friends."

Charlee narrowed her eyes. "Okay, look, if this is some kind of joke, just get on with it."

"What?" Sandra cocked an eyebrow.

"Didn't Tina send you here to make fun of me?"

Sandra choked on a piece of banana and spit it out. "Are you kidding me? You think I'm with that snotty witch? No way, and I'm hurt you'd even think that." She rose from the table.

Charlee regrouped. "No…wait…I'm sorry. It's just that…you're the first person to really talk to me. I would like to be friends."

Sandra sat back down and a smile returned. "Great then." She held a hand out to Charlee. "Like I said, nice to meet you, Charlee."

They shook hands. "Can I ask you just one question?" Charlee asked.

"Yeah."

"Why have you waited until now to talk to me?"

Sandra touched a gold necklace around her neck. A cross was hidden beneath her white T-shirt embroidered with *Peace* in pink letters. "I guess I just woke up today and decided it was time to make a friend. I've kind of flown solo for a long time."

Charlee nodded, her eyes focused on the pendant peeking out from Sandra's shirt. It was simple and faded—not like those shiny, curvy shaped crosses or flowery ones in department stores. It seemed right for Sandra. "That's a nice necklace."

Sandra held up the pendant and rubbed it between her thumb and forefinger. "My grandmother gave it to me. It was hers. She died last year. You know, it's strange but when I wear it, I kind of feel like she's watching over me...protecting me, like a guardian angel."

"I'm sorry she died."

"You say 'sorry' a lot."

"I'm sorr...er...I mean, yeah."

"I would have liked to introduce you to my grandmother." Sandra's smile grew. "She was a lot of fun—really cool, you know. My parents say I'm like her. I hope they're right."

Charlee returned the smile. "I've only known you a few minutes, but you're one of the two coolest people at this table."

"There's no one else...oh, funny." Sandra laughed. Charlee chuckled as well until an unwanted voice brought the moment to a quick end.

"Hey girls, looks like you got yourselves a geeky party going on here."

Charlee closed her eyes and sighed. *Tina!*

"Fatty Smelton has a friend." Tina leaned in and placed her hands on the table. Three golden bracelets clinked together around one of her thin, well-tanned wrists and a gold watch encircled the other. Her right hand cradled an iPhone. "And of course it would be a loser like Sandra Flores. Who else would be your friend?"

Charlee clenched her fists, but it was Sandra who spoke first. "Tina, get over yourself. Why don't you take that little designer outfit and slither away. No one here cares what you have to say."

Tina stood motionless. Her tan skin blushed, her forehead turned fiery red. An eye twitched and her chin trembled. Moments passed before her skin returned to normal, and Tina forced a laugh that sounded like a chicken's cackle. "I get it now. Fatty Smelton has a girly bodyguard. Oh, this is so perfect. Well, I'll leave you two alone now." Walking away, she chuckled and made the gesture of an *L*, the signal for *Losers*. Charlee's gut hurt worse than if Tina had thrown a punch. Sandra was so brave! Why couldn't she be like that?

"Did you see that? Stand up to a bully and they'll back down." Cheer filled Sandra's voice. Charlee didn't answer, didn't even make eye contact with Sandra. She got up from the table, straightened her glasses and grabbed her backpack. "I...I have to go."

"What? Why?"

"I have to study. Maybe I'll see you around." Charlee slung the back-pack over her shoulder then sped off, head bowed. Sandra was just doing what came naturally to her. Charlee knew that. But any shred of coolness she might have had in anyone's eyes was now completely gone because Sandra was the one who shut down Tina. Sandra was not a loser, and she shouldn't be hanging around with one.

Charlee sulked through the rest of the day.

When the final bell signaled the end of school, she walked down the hall, shoulders slouched, head still low.

"Hey! Anyone ever tell you it's not polite to leave a friend alone like that?" Sandra's words echoed down the hall. "Why'd you run off?" She approached with a warm smile that hadn't faded from lunch.

"I'm sorry," Charlee mumbled. "I guess I felt like a geek. I mean, you stood up to Tina, when I was the one she went after. It was me she was trying to hurt. And I don't need a bodyguard."

Sandra grinned. "I know. Listen, next time I won't get in the way. Tina just gets me so mad, and there are so many of us who can't stand her. I don't know why we don't all band together to put the queen and all those other snobs in their place."

"Maybe that day is coming." Charlee lifted her backpack higher up on her shoulder. "In the meantime, if you ever see me getting my butt kicked, feel free to get in the way."

"Deal," Sandra agreed. "Now let's go grab some burgers at M's Diner. It's just four blocks away."

Sandra took hold of Charlee's arm and led her out the front gate of the school. "There's this awesome video game there that I want you to see."

"Great." Charlee stumbled along after Sandra. They raced out the gate until Charlee saw something across the street. A wave of terror, the kind caused by teenage embarrassment, flooded her body.

22

Chapter 5

An Unexpected Visit

Charlee removed her glasses and put them on again, checking the lenses. *It* shouldn't be there—but *it* was. Across the street on the sidewalk next to Mrs. Newman, the old crossing guard, stood the ugly two-wheeler her dad had brought home last night. Its front reflector stared at her.

"Hey, you all right?" Sandra asked.

"Oh…uh…yeah."

"No, really, what's the matter? You just went pale as a ghost."

"N…nothing," Charlee frowned at the bike. "Really, everything's fine."

Sandra whirled her head in the bike's direction. "Are you looking at that bike? Hey, I think it's cool, too. Do you think it's Newman's? I mean, do you think she can even ride a bike? Charlee, you still with me? Earth to Charlee!"

"It's not her bike," Charlee confessed. "It's mine."

"What, really? Well, let's go get it before someone grabs it. You know, you really shouldn't leave cool stuff like that out in the city. It could be stolen." Sandra darted across the street, dodging traffic and ignoring Newman's whistle to stop.

"Sandra, wait!" Charlee followed, hoping no one was watching. Then something Sandra said clicked. *In the city…it could be stolen.* Yes. In the city, anything could be stolen.

"Where'd you get such a retro bike? I mean, this is way cool." Sandra stood over the bike studying each scratch like some archaeologist who had just made a great find. "It's like something from…I don't know…from when our parents were kids. Maybe even before."

"My dad gave it to me."

Sandra raised an eyebrow. "This is great. I wish I had my bike with me. Then we could ride together. Wait, I have an idea. I'll sit on the handlebars, and you can give me a ride to M's."

"I don't think that's such a good idea."

"Sure it is. Hop on and let's go."

Staring at the bike, Charlee hesitated. With a few shallow breaths, her muscles tense, she touched the handlebars. Even before she swung a leg over the frame, the same painful shock she felt the night before made her topple to the cement. She yelped when she landed on the sidewalk, much to the delight of the kids making their way home.

Even Sandra couldn't keep herself from giggling. "What was that?"

Charlee dusted herself off and stood. A numbing, tingly sensation rose from her hands and spread throughout her body. "I…uh…I slipped." She tried to hide the embarrassment but her face felt warm. One thing was for sure. She wasn't about to get on the bike again—not ever. "Maybe we should just walk the bike to M's," Charlee suggested.

"Maybe you're right." A broad smile crossed Sandra's face. "Hey, can I push it?" she asked.

"Uhhhh…well, I think—" Charlee never finished. Sandra grasped the handlebars. Wincing, Charlee expected Sandra to be thrown to the ground by the bike's strange power, but nothing happened. Sandra, untouched by any dose of mysterious energy, walked off toward M's. *What?* Charlee didn't understand. Was she imagining things? Why did she get shocked when she touched the bike?

"Strange," she muttered. "It's just strange."

"You coming?" Sandra called. Charlee ran to catch up with Sandra. Together they walked the four blocks to M's and laughed as they devoured hamburgers, drank orange sodas, and played video games. Charlee's cell phone interrupted them once.

"Charlee, where are you?" her mom asked.

"Sorry, Mom. I forgot to call. I'm with a friend at a place near school called M's. We're playing video games."

Her mom's voice eased. "Oh, a friend. I'm happy for you. All right, well, don't be too late."

Charlee sighed. "I know, Mom. Have to go."

Her mom quickly said, "Love you."

"Love you, too," Charlee whispered in response before placing the phone back in her pocket.

"Your mom checking up on you, huh," Sandra teased.

"Yeah."

"Mine too. I just got a text." The two laughed.

By four o'clock, after playing a few more video games, it was time to part ways. "Charlee, I had fun. Thanks for hanging out." Sandra rose from the table.

"I had fun, too." Charlee took a last gulp of soda before throwing the cup in the trash. "Thanks…for everything."

"What do you mean?"

"Uh…nothing." Charlee silently cursed herself. Those last words sounded a bit too pathetic. She quickly changed subject. "If you want, we can eat lunch together again tomorrow."

"I'd like that." Sandra nodded. "Maybe we can even get in a fight with Tina. We could kick her butt." They laughed some more as they left M's. With a wave, Sandra turned and started home.

Charlee waited until Sandra disappeared around the corner. Turning to the bike, she said, "I don't care if Sandra thinks you're cool. I know the truth. How am I going to get rid of you?" She walked around the bike, thinking as hard as she could. Then she remembered what Sandra had said. *Of Course!* She would leave the bike in an alley somewhere among the nearby neighborhood businesses. Someone would take it, and she would be rid of the bike forever.

The plan was simple. Stash the bike then wander around for an hour. Before going home, mess up her clothes, hair, and muddy her face. Finally, head home and tell Mom and Dad some older kids had jumped her in an alley and taken the bike. Fool-proof.

If her dad felt bad enough, he might even get her a decent bike. But how to get the bike downtown—she didn't dare touch it. *My socks!* She wore ankle-high socks. Charlee removed them and wrapped the socks around her hands. With hands protected, she reached for the handlebars. *Don't hurt me. Don't hurt me. Don't hurt me.*

Charlee stretched out her fingers and grabbed the handlebars, waiting for the stunning sensation to strike. It never came. Other than the strangeness of wearing socks on her hands, everything felt normal. The time had come to implement the plan. She didn't bother riding the bike. She walked it the four blocks to an intersection lined with brick businesses and alleys. Her pace was quick, eyes determined.

When she got to one business, Danny's Pizza & Deli, Charlee felt strangely drawn to it. She stopped at the door-front window, compelled to peek into the deli. Inside, several customers ate while an old man labored behind a counter. Grease covered his apron. She couldn't be sure, but at one point, he seemed to glance her way as he twisted the end of a long, white mustache between his thumb and forefinger.

Charlee shook herself away from the window. What was she doing? *Focus.* She had a mission. She snuck past the pizza-deli shop to an alley beside the business. It would do just fine. Besides, she was tired of walking the bike. The alley had three trash bins, each one overflowing with old bread and pizza boxes. She could hide the bike behind them. If anyone found it, that wouldn't be a problem. No one would know the bike's owner. No one would care. She would leave the bike, walk around for a while, and then head home to shed fake tears over the loss of such a wonderful gift.

Stashing the two-wheeler behind the trash bin farthest from the alley's entrance, she then slipped down the block. After crossing a few intersections, Charlee stopped and rested against a brick wall. No one seemed to be following her. The plan had worked…so far.

For the next hour she wandered around, checking out the window displays at a toy store and purchased a few chocolate balls from a candy shop. At 5:30, her cell rang. It was her mom. She hit the ignore button. *Good*. Her mom was worried. It was time to go home.

The sky dimmed and Charlee began her walk home. At a park just a few blocks away she messed herself up by rolling around in the dirt and grass. She rubbed oil splotches from the street against her arms and clothing to add to the lie. Charlee thought about breaking her glasses but decided against it. No need to go that far. By now she must look like someone who could have been mugged.

A block away from home, Charlee wrestled with how to make herself cry. She finally grabbed a nose hair and pulled. OUCH! Immediately, tears formed. All that remained was to walk inside the house and wait for her mom's relieved hug. Prepared with fake sobs and manufactured tears, Charlee climbed the steps of the front porch and reached for the door. Her mom threw the door open first.

Charlee acted quickly. She grabbed hold of her mom and sobbed, "Mom—"

"Charleya, we have a guest." Her mom spoke with some annoyance—*and used my formal name*—not the expected reaction. Charlee peeked into the house. An unfamiliar, elderly man in a brown sweater sat on the sofa in the family room. He had a wrinkled face with a large white mustache that hid his mouth and he was bald except for a bit of gray hair on the sides of his head. Wait a second, she recognized him.

"Charlee, I'd like you to meet Mr. Daniel Levenstein," her mom said.

"Uh, call me Danny." Mr. Levenstein's body creaked as he lifted himself to shake hands.

"Charlee, Mr. Levenstein owns Danny's Pizza & Deli." Her mom folded her arms. "It seems that your bike ended up in the alley next to his store.

Fortunately, your name and address were on the bike, so he drove it all the way here. Wasn't that nice of him?"

"Yeah." Charlee knew trouble waited, but right now her thoughts focused on how much she despised Mr. Levenstein. And who had put her name and address on the bike? Dad! She twisted a long strand of hair in a tight knot.

"Well, young lady, I'm just glad I was able to find your bike before someone else did." Mr. Levenstein's hazel eyes were round and friendly. "Next time, you must be more careful."

"Yes, sir." She avoided his stare.

"Mr. Levenstein, I'd like to pay you for your time." Her mom reached for her purse.

"Oh no, thank you. I'm just glad I could help."

"What about some coffee, then?"

"Thank you, but I must be getting back to my store. I left my baker in charge and he's bound to burn the place down." He started for the front door, walking with a limp and shoulders hunched.

Charlee watched him then looked down at the carpet. What had she done to this poor man? When she glanced up again, Mr. Levenstein stood beside her. "You should never give up something as valuable as this bike of yours," the old man whispered. "You may find that it is a truly wondrous gift."

Charlee stepped back. How did he know the bike was a gift? What did he mean, wondrous?

"Your mother was telling me that your father brought the bike home for you just yesterday." Offering a final smile, the old man went out the door. On the porch, he stopped one more time and winked at Charlee's mom. The moment didn't last long, but they nodded to each other. That was strange. Did her mom know him?

"Come down to my store some time," Mr. Levenstein offered. "I'll give you a free slice of pizza, or maybe a nice corned beef on rye. Maybe I can tell you stories about the old country."

"Thank you, sir," Charlee said. As much as she wanted to hate him for bringing the bike back, she couldn't. Mr. Levenstein was nice and did a good deed. The fact he spoiled her plans was beside the point. How could he know?

I'm a big fat jerk. She watched the man move down the steps of the porch and limp toward a blue van with "Danny's Pizza & Deli" painted in red letters on the passenger door. When the old man drove away, Charlee turned to her mom.

27

"You have a lot of explaining to do," her mom scolded. "It's a good thing your father's department called a meeting tonight. He would have been so hurt by this."

"Mom—"

"Your bike is on the side of the house. Please put it in the garage."

Charlee nodded.

Her mom then softened. "Charlee, I know you're going through changes, I mean what with the move and the new school. Just remember, if you find yourself facing challenges, you may feel alone, but you're not. You'll never be alone, no matter what. Remember that. Always remember that." Charlee's mom hugged her tightly then released the embrace, keeping one hand on her shoulder. "If you ever need to talk, I'm here for you. Would you like to talk now?"

"No. It's late, and I have homework. Maybe tomorrow." Charlee stomped off toward the bike. There, under a hazy purple evening sky stood the two-wheeled enemy. She circled it and realized the inescapable truth. She was stuck with this mysterious reject bike.

Chapter 6

The Dream Returns

Charlee dreamt again. She had gone to sleep around nine o'clock as punishment for ditching the bike. Now, like the dream from last night, she wore the scratchy brown clothing instead of pajamas. The same sword hung at her waist. New to the ensemble was a long, wooden bow resting over one shoulder and a satchel containing a dozen arrows strapped to her back.

"This is just too weird." Though she wore the same clothing, she no longer stood on a pathway lined by trees under a canopy of branches that hid the sunlight.

Charlee was atop a mountain overlooking a valley where fields of blue grass stretched across the landscape. Massive trees with corkscrew shaped trunks spiraled toward a cloudless emerald sky. The trees dwarfed the red woods of Yosemite National Park where her family had once driven their car through a cutout tree trunk.

Across the valley was a colossal structure that snaked over the land for miles. Charlee strained for a better look.

"I think it's a wall," she uttered out loud. Staring at it, she was reminded of The Great Wall of China. Charlee stood on her tiptoes, which gave her a better view. Beyond the wall was a sprawling city nestled against the mountain range. A castle built into a mountainside cast a wide shadow over the land.

"What am—" Over her shoulder, creatures broke out in a song of mixed warbles and hoots. Charlee peered up and spied winged songsters soaring by. They were much larger than any birds she had ever seen. Like smaller versions of a giraffe, they had long, spotted necks, snouts, and four legs—two of which ended in bird-like claws rather than hooves. Their rainbow-colored wings extended maybe a car's length on either side.

"Amazing, aren't they?"

Charlee whirled around to face one of the winged giraffes. Its body her height, but the head rose several feet above her.

"Don't be afraid," the creature urged. "You will receive no harm—at least not from me. I am Saur."

The creature spoke an inhuman language, just as the leaves had in the earlier dream, but this was different. A series of screeches and caws formed words. She somehow understood the meaning of each distinctive sound and managed to respond. "I…I am Charlee," she screeched.

"It is my pleasure to meet you, Charlee." The creature, Saur, gracefully bowed its long neck.

Off in the distance, beyond the flying herd, water gently flowed. She remembered the creek and the woman floating in the water. Memories of the giant hooded man invaded her thoughts. This wasn't the same place as the earlier dream, and that couldn't be the same body of water, or could it? Still, this mountain and the valley below felt shrouded in a desperate winter frost despite the sun's warmth. *It's still just a dream*, she reminded herself. *Nothing to really fear.* Yet, fear swept over her like an ocean wave.

"You seem distracted. Are you all right, child?" Saur asked.

She wasn't. She wanted to get back home…or wake up. "Saur, where am I? What is this place?"

"It is your home," Saur answered.

"I…I don't understand."

"You will."

"Do all things in this forest speak?" Charlee asked.

"That is an odd question. All beings have a language, if you are willing to listen." The winged creature tilted its head and blinked green eyes, which seemed wise but tired.

"This dream…whatever it is…feels so real." Charlee listened as the leaves from nearby trees whispered, but she couldn't quite make out their conversation. "Why do I keep coming here?"

"It was once a place of great joy." Saur spread his wings.

"What do you—"

A familiar haunting song returned. Could it be the woman she had seen before? Charlee tried to find where the song was coming from but when she turned back to Saur, the creature had taken flight and hovered overhead. "Wait! Don't leave," Charlee begged, still in Saur's language.

"I cannot say more. I must be going. Soar with caution." The creature rose into the sky and disappeared with the others of his kind.

Again Charlee listened for the melody and shuddered. If the woman was nearby, the giant man might be as well. "I don't want to face him again. But if this is really a dream, why fear the giant?"

She stumbled forward toward the sound of sloshing water. Before, she had dreamt of a creek by a tree-lined path. Now, she moved toward a body of water atop a mountain. Was it because in the real world she had to go to the bathroom? That thought made her laugh and eased her nerves…momentarily.

With each step the song grew louder. As Charlee listened, she realized something. Though sung in an unfamiliar language, she understood the words—just as she understood the leaf creatures and Saur.

Oh sweet water, wash away the pain that would sweep me away, for I cannot bear the loss of loved ones whom evil from me would tear and bring to me a hero who will stand for good and with the power only a hero can command deliver me to safe lands.

"So much pain," Charlee said. "She sounds sad, like she really does need help."

Pushing on, she reached a gathering of trees with low-hanging branches covered with the pulsating star-shaped leaves. As she pressed forward through the foliage, the leaves whispered what felt like a warning. Charlee froze. The giant might be close. She placed her hand on the sword at her side and listened. Nothing. Peering over her shoulder revealed no signs of danger.

"Come on, don't stop now. Be brave," she told herself.

The song grew louder and Charlee dashed ahead, ducking branches and jumping over brush. When she reached a clearing she lowered to her knees and kept hidden behind the trees. Below her, a hillside dropped toward a narrow waterway with banks about a stone's throw apart. The woman was at the water's edge, sitting atop a boulder surrounded by tall grass. Long glowing hair covered the woman's shoulders and tumbled down her back. Sunlight gleamed off something atop her head. "A crown! She must be some princess or maybe a queen."

"You there among the trees—who's there?" the woman unexpectedly asked without turning away from the water. "I will be most frightened if you do not speak up."

Charlee crouched. *What a doofus.* Lost in thought, she had strayed from the cover of the greenery. *Now what? Introduce yourself?*

"Please show yourself." The woman stood and scanned the trees.

With a long sigh, Charlee rose and started down the hillside until a tug on her shirt stopped her. *Oh no, the giant!* Her face went cold, like when the blood rushed from her head on a roller coaster that flipped her upside down last year at the fair.

"Please don't hurt me?" she pleaded.

No response followed. Heart racing, breaths shallow, she turned to face her captor. Instead, her shirt had snagged on a tree branch. Strange though, it felt like the tree branch had reached out to ensnare her. It wouldn't let go. Struggling to break free, a thousand little leaf voices whispered at once: *Turn back!*

Their advice had to be about the giant man, but since she didn't see him she ignored their advice. Nevertheless, she would remain vigilant. Faced flushed with embarrassment, Charlee continued down the hillside toward the woman.

"Well, there you are!" The young woman, maybe in her twenties, glided through a thicket of brush and moved nimbly up to greet Charlee. She wore a white dress with a golden belt wrapped around her waist and the crown, simple but elegant, showed through her long blonde hair like a tiara. "You are the one who has been watching me."

"Yes…I mean no. I wasn't spying." Charlee peered up at the woman, who stood a couple of feet taller. The woman spoke the same language as in the song. Charlee understood the words as if having learned them long ago but forgotten. The language had a name—Lengoron. How did she know that?

Charlee's gaze focused on the woman's striking features—her flawless pale skin, high cheekbones and large lips—features that would have made her popular with bully Tina Lomeli. The woman was like a fairy—more than human. Her crystal eyes stood out the most. Just like Charlee's little sister.

"Who might you be? And why were you watching me?" The woman seemed to chant as she spoke. Each word flowed from her tongue as if spoken in a melody.

"Uh…" Charlee backed away.

"You carry the weapons of a knight, and though I have seen young women serve as knights, I have never seen one as young as you. What crown do you serve?"

Charlee pondered, but her mind went blank. "Huh?"

"Are you from afar?"

"Yes, from a land far away—far, far, far away."

"Woman, get away from the girl!" The gruff command came from the clearing up the hill. There stood the giant man, draped in his black cloak.

The woman moved in close, gripping Charlee's arm. "Protect me, young knight!" Her touch burned, like an ice cube left on the skin too long. Charlee shuddered but otherwise ignored the pain. It was just a dream.

"Woman, get away from the girl. Now!" the giant man again commanded.

He threw off the hood, revealing a scarred face, chiseled and leathery. The eyes, deep-set black orbs, were stained with blood. His red beard tinted with gray ended in a jagged point at his chest.

"Please, young knight," the woman whispered. "It is your duty to protect me."

"You are not going to harm her." Charlee's knees trembled but she reached for her sword to unsheathe it. The blade was heavy and even though she held it with two hands, the sword drooped.

"Young fool!" Clearly, the giant was not impressed. He strode forward on tree-trunk-sized legs.

"You...you'll have to fight me," Charlee threatened. "I mean it."

"So be it." The giant man raised his sword.

Chapter 7

A Girl and Her Bike

Ahhhh!" Charlee tumbled out of bed onto the floor. Once the fogginess and confusion of the dream cleared, she unfroze one body part at a time and then stood. Breathing more calmly, she realized she still wore the superman T-shirt and pajama bottoms. Actually, they never really disappeared because, again, it was a dream. Charlee peeked at the clock on the nightstand.

Midnight.

Parched, she decided to dare the long walk through the quiet house for a soda. Charlee loved soft drinks. Something about the fizzle and spray was comforting. Reaching for her glasses atop the nightstand, she placed them on her face and slipped into a pair of open-toe sandals. Pushing hair from her face, she tiptoed to the door across her plush carpet, which was comforting, too. It felt real and right now *real* mattered. Once at the door, she opened it and peered into the hallway. The house was dark but no signs of trouble appeared.

You can do it. She urged herself forward even as she shivered against the sensation of a thousand pins and needles. *It was just a dream*, she reminded herself one more time. *You're in your own house. Don't be a scared baby.* She ventured down the hallway, stopping at the top of the stairs just long enough to release a breath of air and didn't stop again until reaching the kitchen.

There, Charlee flipped on the light and threw open the refrigerator. A gallon of milk strategically hid the soda. Skipping a glass, Charlee took a swig from the bottle and enjoyed a mouthful of the sweet, fizzy nectar. She lifted the bottle again for another drink, but something knocked the bottle away. Soda splashed across the floor. Heart pounding in her chest like a drum, Charlee stepped away from the fallen soda until the same force ensnared her in a grip as if invisible hands grasped her arms. *What now? This can't be real! I'm losing my mind!*

Just like popular ghost movies where people are unexpectedly tossed about like rag dolls, the force, or spirit, or whatever it was, lifted Charlee and carried her from the kitchen.

"No, help me!" she tried to scream, but something muzzled the words. She reached for the countertop and strained to hold on but couldn't. *Leave me alone!*

Whatever it was propelled Charlee toward the garage. Her eyes bulged as the door swung open on its own. *Mom...help me!* Charlee floated through the doorway, down the steps to the garage, which, unlike the rest of the house, blazed in a blinding white light.

Covering her eyes, Charlee screamed silently—her voice still muzzled as if her mouth had been gagged. *Let me go!* The unseen force responded, lowering her to the ground and releasing its grip. Charlee was free. She could run but she didn't. Something inside her compelled her to stay. Dropping her hands from her eyes as the light faded to a gentle glow, Charlee scanned the garage for the light source. She found it quickly. In the corner awash in a white radiance was the bike.

"I should have known," she stuttered as she swallowed a load of saliva and forced her legs to be still. Charlee hated the old two-wheeler from the moment she laid eyes on it. She tried without success to be rid of it. Now, as she eyed the bike, its frame pulsating with white energy, she understood. No matter how much she might hate the bike, it was like no other cruiser, dirt bike, mountain bike, or ten-speed she could buy in a store. This bike was special and it wanted something. She just wasn't sure what.

Chapter 8

Okay, Bike. Now What?

Charlee stepped cautiously to the glowing two-wheeler. "Okay, bike. I'm here. What do you want?" The bike remained motionless, silent. Its pulsating glow surrounded Charlee.

"Hey bike, remember all those mean things I said about you? Can we forget about that? I didn't mean it. Sorry for ditching you in the alley. Let's just be friends. I'm about to put my hands on you. Please don't hurt me."

Teeth clenched in preparation of the jolt sure to come, she reached for the bike with both hands. She counted down—*three...two...one*—then her hands grasped the handlebars. Nothing! No lightning strike. No explosion. Nothing happened at all. The chrome felt warm, as if the bike had been left outside on a hot summer day. Other than that, life seemed unchanged.

Charlee glared at the bike. The glowing light had disappeared, and she stood in the garage, gripping the most hideous bike ever. "Did I imagine everything? Was I sleepwalking? Am I asleep right now in my bed? Is this part of a dream?"

She swung her leg over the frame and sat on the banana seat...maybe to tempt fate. More warmth rose throughout her body, but still no stinging burst of energy to signal the start of some momentous change. "Dumb bike. What a joke! You're nothing but a pile of rusting—"

Her words vanished when the garage door slid open on its own, revealing a sleeping street in the dark hours of early morning. *No, not again!* Outside, a light breeze ruffled the leaves in the trees. From the distance came the screech of fighting cats. Except for these sounds, stillness filled the night.

"Okay. This is very weird and very wrong. Wrong, wrong, wrong! This can't be happening. There's no way. I must be dreaming. That's it. I'm dreaming—and now I'd like to wake up, please." Charlee pinched herself. Nothing changed. She remained in the garage on the bike, staring at the street. "Listen, bike. This has been fun and all, but I think I'm going to go back inside now. Okay?"

But slowly, with Charlee still on the banana seat, the bike rolled out of the garage, down the driveway, and onto the sidewalk. She tried to lift her hands from the handlebars, but…*they're stuck*! She braced her feet on the cement but the bike kept moving forward.

"Mom, Dad…help me!" she cried, but her words echoed back at her as if they had bounced off some invisible force field. "Anyone, please help!" Again her words hit an unseen wall, like she was in some kind of box surrounding her and the bike.

Charlee wrestled to free her hands. "Bike, let me go! I promise I won't say another mean thing about you. I'll ride you to school every day. I'll clean you. I'll make sure your chain is greased. Just stop."

The bike came to a stop in the street and finally she was able to let go. "All right, bike. I'm just going to get off slowly and then I'll take you back into the garage. We'll both get some sleep and tomorrow we can go to school together." She smiled nervously. "Doesn't that sound ni—"

Like a bullet the bike shot forward. Charlee strained against the G-forces, which were stronger than in any roller coaster she'd ever ridden. Her vision tunneled in on itself. She was blacking out.

"What's happening?" The onrushing wind swallowed the words. The bike zipped down the street—past one block, then another and another. They raced up steep-hilled streets, jumping at the peaks, and flying down the other sides. She fought to keep her eyes open against the dizzying streaks of light rushing by. Queasiness set in. Charlee's stomach rolled over and over. She was going to be sick.

"Stop!" she shouted. The bike heeded her command. Just as suddenly as the ride began, it ended. Charlee's feet flew above her head as she flipped over the handlebars. Her body slammed against the cold, unforgiving pavement and rolled several times before coming to a stop.

"Owww!" She lay on the cement staring up at the night sky watching the stars spin. The vomit came in disgusting bursts. When it was over, she rolled back and closed her eyes. She didn't open them again until the world stopped spinning. After the nausea subsided, Charlee stood on wobbly legs. When another bout of nausea returned she hunched over and spotted her glasses on the sidewalk.

She chuckled weakly. "They must have blown off my face."

Charlee bent down to pick them up and placed them back atop her nose, but the lenses must have cracked or been scratched. Everything looked fuzzy. She checked her glasses for any breaks but other than a few spots of dirt they were fine. Placing them back on her face, the hazy vision returned.

"Wait a second." She lifted away the glasses and the world around was clear. "Very weird."

Charlee staggered to the bike. "Wh…what's going on here? Are you trying to get back at me? Is that what this is? You know, you could have at least let me put on my clothes. You think I want the world to see me in my pajamas?"

The bike stared with its front reflector. Did she expect a response? Anything was possible. This was no ordinary bike. Maybe it could talk. Maybe it could explain for what purpose it had dragged her out here in the middle of the night.

Charlee's eyes swept over the street. It was a more affluent neighborhood. The homes here were large, many gated. The neighborhood was asleep except for the pale glow cast by lamp posts. "What is it, bike? Why are we here?" The bike stood silent.

She placed a hand on the banana seat, triggering a new sensation. Instead of a painful zap, she felt invigorated—even powerful. She was more alert, her senses heightened. Placing the glasses in her pajama pocket, she surveyed the neighborhood with eyes that saw sharper than they ever did even with glasses. Staring down the street, Charlee could read the license plate number of a car parked eight houses away, make out the tiny lettering of a family's last name over a doorway ten houses down, and spot the yellow eyes of a cat peeking from underneath a pickup two blocks away.

Charlee gasped. More changes followed. She heard things—not just rustling leaves or dogs barking in the distance, but sounds no normal human ear would be able to detect from where she stood—a man snoring in his bed, a baby breathing deeply in its crib and a caterpillar inching up a tree.

Then…footsteps! Someone was slipping through the backyard of the house across the street.

"Bike, maybe it's just someone locked out of their house." She listened again and reached a different conclusion as she heard tools clanging in a bag slung across the intruder's back.

Charlee removed her hand from the bike seat. The sounds disappeared, but the sense of trouble remained. "I think someone's about to break into that house. But what if I'm wrong? I can't just start shouting and wake up everybody on this street. They'd think I was a lunatic or something. I'd be in trouble for sure. Is this why you brought me here? What am I supposed to do?"

She reached for a cell phone but remembered she hadn't brought it. "I could have made a call to the police if I had remembered my cell phone. See, bike, you should have let me get my head straight before bringing me out here."

39

She paced back and forth. "What am I supposed to do? Can I trust my senses? Can I trust the bike? No! Before I do anything, I need proof."

Charlee sprinted across the street to the house where she'd heard the suspicious noises. At the front yard, she slowed and tiptoed up to the fence that ran along the side of the house. What was she doing? She should turn around and walk home. Leave the bike here.

As if she were someone else—someone braver—Charlee opened the fence and slowly crept to the back of the house, body pressed up against the wall's rough surface. *Please don't let a thief be here. Let me be wrong.* Her heart sank when she spied the outlines of a large man kneeling at the back door of the house. It looked like he was trying to cut some kind of wire, perhaps to an alarm system. Any minute now, the unwanted night visitor would break in. She couldn't let that happen.

But what could she do—scream? That would alert everyone inside of the danger. Sure, it wasn't exactly what a hero would do, but maybe the man would be frightened and run away. She flattened against the wall and prepared to belt out the loudest scream she had. Unfortunately, at that moment something else caught her attention—something huge with eight spindly legs.

The spider crawled from the wall onto Charlee's shoulder and then onto her neck. As the first spidery legs touched skin, she spun in a wild dance to shake off the creature. Mistake! Charlee jumped away from the wall and stood in full view.

She hoped the prowler's attention had been focused elsewhere but it hadn't. He rose to his feet then scrambled toward her, a long, silvery wrench clutched tightly in a black gloved hand. *Scream now!* But she couldn't even swallow. She just stared.

The man, dressed in black, from his sweatpants to his sweatshirt all the way up to the ski mask over his face, stopped just a couple of steps away.

Think fast! "Uh, is this the Peterson house?" Charlee whispered. "I have a pizza delivery." The masked man just stood there, his head tilted. "I guess not," Charlee backed away. "I guess I got the wrong house. Sorry. I'll be going now."

"I don't think so." The man spoke in a throaty, threatening voice. He took a step forward, still clutching the wrench.

"I'll yell," Charlee warned. "Everyone will hear and come running."

The man clearly had no fear of a thirteen-year-old girl in pajamas. He smiled through a hole cut in the ski mask, exposing yellow teeth that glowed in the night. "Do it, kid, and it'll be the last sound you ever make. I've killed before and I can do it again. Go ahead, scream."

Shivering with fear, Charlee struggled just to breathe. How did she get herself into this? How would she get herself out of this? She tried to scream, "Help!" It came out as barely a squeak.

The would-be thief raised the wrench over his head. "Sorry, kid. I can't have any witnesses."

Charlee tripped over her own feet and toppled to the grass. At that moment she did the only thing she could think of. In a shaky voice, just above a whisper, she called to the two-wheeler. "Bike, I need your help—now!"

"Get up!" The man reached down with his free hand and clasped Charlee's arm. "This will teach...wait, what the—"

The bike—that ugly scrap of metal—charged through the side gate and before the man had time to react crashed into him. The burglar was knocked off his feet, landing with a thud on his back.

Dazed, he lifted himself to his knees. "What...what happened?" Shaking off his confusion, he stood with the wrench still in hand. "I'm going to get you, kid!" Before reaching his full height, the bike rushed at him again. The burglar flew across the yard and smashed against the wooden fence before falling face down to the ground. A soft groan escaped his lips then he lay silent.

For a heartbeat, Charlee stared at the bike. It waited, supported by its kickstand. When she could finally move she picked herself up, tiptoed over to the man, and checked to see if he breathed. He did. The bike had knocked him unconscious.

"The bike just saved my life." She contemplated the bike in disbelief. "Thanks!"

A light went on inside the house then the light in the back porch blazed to life. The residents had heard the commotion and were coming out. Charlee ran to the bike and leaped on the banana seat just as the back door slid open and a heavy, balding man in a robe emerged. He held a baseball bat. "What in the world is going on here?" The bat was poised over his shoulder.

"Everything's all right, sir. This man was going to break into your house." Charlee toughened her voice and pointed at the unconscious thief. "But I...I mean...we...stopped him. You should call the police before he wakes up."

A plump woman in curlers rushed out. "Harvey, what's going on?"

"Nancy, go inside and call the police," Harvey ordered.

"Who is this girl?" Nancy asked, her eyes fixed on Charlee.

"I don't know, but I think she just stopped that man from robbing us." Harvey pointed the bat at the unconscious man. For the first time, the woman looked at the dark lump lying motionless on the ground. "Oh, my!"

41

"Hon, please go call the police."

She disappeared into the house.

Harvey continued to regard Charlee. "Well, who are you?"

Charlee thought about that for a moment. She wasn't sure how to answer. She couldn't give her name. She wanted to give a heroic response, but in the end simply said, "I'm just a friend."

"Harvey, the police are on their way," Nancy said from inside the house.

"Good," Charlee responded. "I'll be leaving now."

With a nod to Harvey, she called, "Bike, let's ride!" The bike scurried from the backyard through the side gate. They rushed to the end of the block and stopped. There, Charlee used her enhanced hearing to listen for sirens and a few minutes later, they were off in the distance. Charlee focused her hearing one more time on the burglar. He still hadn't stirred. "Good, we can go," Charlee told the bike. "Let's not be around when the police get here. I'm not quite sure how to explain all this."

Apparently, the bike agreed. It bolted away from the neighborhood at unnaturally high speeds, rocketing past homes and cars. Gripping the handlebar to hang on, Charlee leaned into the rushing wind. She sensed the night was just beginning.

Chapter 9

The Next Rescue

As they whizzed past one block after the other, Charlee became accustomed to the momentum. Vision in focus, hands and feet relaxed, she could steer the bike, decide its direction. It was as if the rest of the world moved in slow motion. Still, she let the bike set their course. If the bike had some grand plan, she would trust it—for now.

She closed her eyes and felt the wind toss and whip her hair. She breathed in the crisp night air and the city's scents flowed through her nostrils from the mustiness of the Bay to the smell of pork fried rice in Chinatown, also too far away for a normal nose to sense. Her plump arms, which had never touched weights or done much in the way of exercise, flexed with new-found strength as if she were like those power lifters from the Olympics.

"What's happening to me?" she asked.

Charlee stared at the bike from the tires, little more than rotating blurs, to the scratched and nicked white frame. "What is this two-wheeled heap I'm trusting to take me wherever it wants?" she questioned herself. "Something is going on I haven't figured out yet, but tonight I just want to ride. Tonight I just want to be a superhero."

The bike carried her to a familiar street filled with businesses. Oddly enough, they stopped in front of Danny's Pizza & Deli, the restaurant owned by Mr. Levenstein who had returned the bike after Charlee stashed it in his alley. "This is where I tried to ditch you earlier. Why did you bring me here?"

Aging brick shops crowded together festooned with neon signs that softly hummed in unison. Unlike the pale illumination of the residential neighborhoods, the lights soaked the businesses in colors that alternated from green to red, blue to yellow and back again.

This part of the city had closed for the night, except for a scattering of late-night cafes and coffee houses. Off in the distance, in the financial district, skyscrapers lit up the darkened sky.

Charlee inspected the street for signs of trouble. A few people walked along the sidewalk, but little else caught her attention—until a voice penetrated the quiet. "You don't have to do this." The words drifted from the alley beside Mr. Levenstein's shop. The voice belonged to...*Mr. Levenstein!*

Pedaling forward, she peeked into a murky alley. Charlee closed her eyes, concentrated, and opened them again. The alley blazed to life as if someone had ignited a spotlight. The overflowing trash, the stray cats hidden under a trash bin, and the cobwebs draped along walls all became visible as shadows vanished. Charlee understood why. *The bike!* With its unexplained power, it gave her super vision, or something close to it. Somehow, contact with the bike changed her.

Inside the alley, Mr. Levenstein stood with two others who clearly meant to harm the old man. One, tall and thin, held a knife with a long blade while the other, short and stocky, clenched a tire iron. The short one did all the talking in a high-pitched squeaky voice. He had to be the leader.

"Leavin' late tonight, old man? We know you keep a bundle of cash in that safe in your back room. Now, open up the door, give us the combination, and we won't hurt you. Say no, and you won't be openin' tomorrow—or any other time."

"Listen, young man. Think about what you're doing." Charlee marveled at the calm in Mr. Levenstein's voice. "If you need money or food, I'd be happy to help you. But this is the wrong path for both of you."

"Shut up!" the leader ordered. He held the tire iron high, ready to bring it crashing down on Mr. Levenstein's head. "We don't want your handouts. We want all your cash." He grabbed Mr. Levenstein's collar with his free hand then shoved the old man back against a crate.

Instead of falling, Mr. Levenstein quickly regained his balance. "Again, I implore you lads to reconsider. If only you would step inside and talk with me over a pizza."

"That does it!" the attacker's voice cracked. "I warned you!"

Charlee's pulse quickened, face burned, and hands formed into fists. How dare these two punks threaten Mr. Levenstein! "Okay, bike. What's our plan?" There was no response. "I wish you could talk. All right, just be ready." She pedaled into the alley. "Get away from him!"

The two snapped their heads around. "What? Who's there? Whoever it is...you best get out of here or you're gonna get hurt!" the short one threatened. He had a rounded face and chiseled little features adorned by a thin mustache and goatee. Eyes bulged from their sockets.

"I said, leave him alone," Charlee commanded.

"Is that a little girl I hear…on a bike?" the tall man chuckled. "What ya doin' here, little girl?"

These were the first words Charlee had heard from him. The thick, raspy voice sent chills up and down her back. His face had a scar along the left cheek, and some of his front teeth were missing. Stubble covered his chin.

Charlee swallowed some spit. What was she doing? She wasn't really a superhero—just a nerdy teenage girl. These men weren't playing a game. They could hurt her. She had gotten lucky before with the burglar, but that knife was no joke. "Bike, we have to get out of here?" she whispered as sweat poured from her brow. The bike didn't budge. She could still run away—leave the bike to fight this battle. Charlee shook her head. *No, we have to help Mr. Levenstein,* she realized. "I'll say it one more time," she pressed. "Leave that man alone!"

"Or what?" the taller man scoffed.

"Or you'll suffer the wrath of…of justice." Charlee cringed. The words had come from a comic book she remembered. *Stupid thing to say.* Not surprisingly, the two laughed and refocused their attention on Mr. Levenstein.

Words failed. It was time to act. The bike stormed toward the two men. Just before it reached them, the bike skidded sideways, ramming into them. They tumbled to the wet cement but recovered quickly.

"You're dead, ya hear me?" With the tire iron in his hand, the leader rose to his feet. His taller partner also got up. He still held the knife. "Get her!" They rushed at her.

No, they're coming! Charlee fumbled to find the pedals, but the bike didn't wait. It leaped into the air, forcing her to hug the frame or be thrown off. Still airborne, the bike spun like a helicopter blade, crashing its tires into the faces of the two attackers. The front tire pummeled them—then the back tire—then the front once more. Thrown backward, they crashed against a brick wall then slid into a trash bin.

The spinning stopped and the bike landed softly on the ground. Her head still spinning, Charlee maintained a grip on the frame. To let go would mean tumbling to the cement and giving in to queasiness. She couldn't throw up a second time tonight, not in front of Mr. Levenstein.

Sucking in a lungful of air, she turned to the old man. "Sir, are you all right?" Charlee deepened her voice and retreated to the alley's edge.

"A little shaken, that's all." Mr. Levenstein rubbed his neck. "Thank you for your help, young lady."

Charlee gulped. *He knows who I am!* She covered her face with her hair then glanced at the attackers. They were unconscious but they would awaken soon. "You should probably call the police."

"Good idea." Mr. Levenstein disappeared into his shop.

Charlee kept watch over the two punks. Their legs dangled over the edge of the trash bin. She couldn't help but smile, patting the bike's handlebars.

"The police are on their way," Mr. Levenstein said, re-emerging in the alley. Then he approached her. "I know you, don't I?"

"Stay where you are." Charlee backed away. "I...I don't think we've ever met."

"No, you're that young—"

Sirens in the night signaled it was time to go.

"The police are on their way." Charlee still spoke in a disguised voice. "I've done my work here. I'll be going now."

"Wait," Mr. Levenstein pleaded. "Don't leave. Let me make you a pizza or a pastrami sandwich to thank you. It's the least I can do."

"Next time. I really must be going." The bike rolled from the alley, but Charlee pulled hard on the brakes. "Sir, I just wanted to say...you're really brave. I hope that someday I can be like you."

"But you are," Mr. Levenstein offered.

"No, not yet. But I hope to be." With that, she rode off into the night. They sped toward their next destination. Charlee wasn't sure what that would be, but she didn't care. *This is amazing!*

Chapter 10

The Pursuit

They stopped next in the financial district, close to the Bay. Rows of skyscrapers lined the streets and stretched to the water's edge. Here, even late at night, the city teemed with life. Horns blared rhythmically. Thousands of voices mixed together from the crowds that filled the streets. No one seemed to care about the late hour.

Charlee craned her neck skyward at the towering skyscrapers, following the contour of the massive buildings to their peaks. She blinked and shook away dizziness.

What were they doing here? After all, bad things happened in this massive part of the city. What could she possibly do about any of it? "Bike, are you sure you came to the right place? Maybe we should go patrol another neighborhood or something."

Not surprisingly, there was no response—at least, not from the bike.

A loud pop, much like the backfire from an old pickup, echoed up and down the street. Startled, Charlee lost balance then tumbled to the sidewalk. The bike landed on top of her. She laughed until a second bang, this time much like a gunshot, traveled up the street followed by another. Sirens, lots of them, blared. Speeding vehicles roared in her direction. She spied the vehicles still blocks down the street. A single sports car weaved in and out of traffic followed by police.

Had the bike come to stop this fast, dangerous pursuit? She stood just as the pursuit zipped by. Her vision slowed down the images enough to allow a careful look at the one leading the chase. It was one of those souped-up sports cars, cherry red with a ridiculously high spoiler. Three men sat inside the vehicle laughing. One waved a handgun out the rear window.

"Bi...bike, I'm not sure about this," Charlee stuttered. Despite her doubt, she jumped back onto the banana seat and the bike blasted forward to join the pursuit. "This is crazy! How are we supposed to stop this?"

Glancing up, Charlee glimpsed a young woman fall into the street ahead of the pursuit. She had been pushed into the path by the crowds straining for a view of the oncoming excitement.

"Bike, faster!" Charlee shouted. The bike charged forward as though slung by a slingshot. It carried them past the police and drew them even with the fleeing sports car. Charlee leaned forward, her chin nearly resting on the handlebars. She urged the bike on until it had surged a few lengths ahead. Just in front of them, the woman lay in the street, frozen. Those on the sidewalk extended their hands to her, but they would not be fast enough.

Seconds remained. "Bike, we have one chance!" They streaked into the intersection. With unexpected strength, Charlee reached down and hooked an arm around the woman's waist. "Now!" The bike swerved away from the pursuit just as the sports car and the chasing police blew by. The quick maneuver caused the bike to slide out from underneath Charlee and she and the woman tumbled to the street.

Darkness swallowed Charlee until voices filtered through the haze. What were they saying? "Did you see that?"…"I can't believe what she just did."…"It's a miracle."…"Is she all right?"…"Give her room to breathe."… "She's coming to."

Charlee slowly opened heavy eyes. She struggled to focus, but as the fogginess broke, the scene cleared. Dozens crowded around. A few knelt over her. "Kid, you okay?"…"Someone call an ambulance!"…"This girl's a hero."

Charlee's mind raced. What was she doing on the ground? What just happened? Did she fall from the bike? Where's the woman? Had she saved her? Shaky, she climbed to her feet. A chorus of applause followed as she stood. "The woman…is she…?" Charlee began to ask.

A man answered, "She's fine. You saved her."

"Where…where is she?"

"There." He pointed to the sidewalk where the woman Charlee rescued sat with others kneeling over her. "But I don't think you should move. You've had a bad fall, and you have a large gash on your forehead. It's bleeding pretty good. An ambulance is on the way."

Charlee touched her forehead, wincing as fingertips felt the warmth of blood. She couldn't wait for an ambulance. Too many questions would be asked. She had to flee but not before making sure the woman was all right. Stumbling through the crowd, Charlee reached her. "Are you okay?"

Someone had draped a sweater around her. Her dress was torn down the right leg, but otherwise she didn't look hurt. "Yes." She didn't bother to look up. Charlee touched her shoulder and then the woman glanced up and smiled, but her gaze never focused. *She's blind.*

"This is the girl who saved you, Meredith." Charlee took a mental note—the woman she helped was named Meredith. A woman tending to Meredith blinked away tears and shook Charlee's hand.

"Emily, help me up." Meredith grimaced as she struggled to stand. Her right ankle buckled, but Emily supported her. Meredith softly touched Charlee's face. "Thank you. Thank you for my life. I was out for the night with my friends, and I don't know what happened."

"I'll tell you what happened," Emily answered. "These Neanderthals were so bent on watching the chase that—"

"I'm sorry you're hurt," Charlee interrupted. "Take care of that ankle." She backed away from Meredith and the crowd.

"What's your name?" Meredith asked. Charlee hesitated. Still woozy, head pounding, she remained aware enough to know this was not the time to be identified—especially while in a Superman T-shirt and pajama bottoms.

Two more gunshots boomed in the distance. The chase wasn't over. *We have to stop them. Bike! Wait, where's my bike?* Charlee whirled in each direction, eyes wide, stomach knotted. "Bike!"

A man wheeled the bike from the street. "Here's your bike, but you really shouldn't ride it right now. You're hurt."

Charlee grabbed the bike and held it close as if she were in a sinking boat and the bike her life raft. "I'm okay," she lied.

Swinging a leg over the frame and climbing onto the seat, she suppressed a scream from the pain that radiated through each limb. With the crowd cheering, Charlee and the bike zoomed off into the night to rejoin the pursuit. They hurried along the center of the street, steering a path through vehicles that pulled to either side of the road as they passed. "Uh, bike, maybe this isn't such a good idea. Maybe we should just let the police handle this. I think we've done enough for one night."

Still in silence, the bike dodged car after car. Up ahead, the lights of the police units flashed. Sirens blared. Gunshots cracked. Thunderous engines echoed through the city streets. How were they going to stop this?

The bike pulled alongside one of the police cars, allowing Charlee a view of the officer driving the unit. When the police officer caught a glimpse of her and the bike, his eyes bulged and his mouth dropped.

Charlee nodded. The bike flew by the squad car and all the others on its way to the vehicle leading the chase. What was the bike going to do?

Was it waiting for her to decide? They quickly reached the sports car. Once more, she eyed the three men inside. They were young and unshaven. They shouted howls of delight; they were not about to surrender. When they noticed her, their eyes widened—just like the officer.

"Pull over!" Charlee pointed at the three. They laughed even harder. "Pull over!" She shook a fist at them.

This time, the man in the back passenger seat pointed his handgun at her. But before the gunman pulled the trigger, the bike surged ahead one car length, then two…three…four. When far ahead of the chase, the bike stopped abruptly in the middle of the street—in the path of the pursuit.

"Bike, what—"

Before she had time to scream, the sports car roared upon them. The bike didn't budge. Charlee ducked under the handlebars. She could no sooner explain what happened next than she could anything that had happened tonight. Just a few feet in front of the bike, the car seemed to smash into an invisible barrier. It flipped over, soaring what seemed almost the length of a school bus before it struck ground again, rolling several times. When it stopped, all that remained was a twisted mess of metal and glass. The men inside moaned.

The chase was over.

Charlee raised her head above the handlebars as patrol cars skidded to a stop and uniformed officers approached the wreck with guns drawn.

"Are you okay?" a voice asked from behind. Frightened, she nearly jumped off the bike. Charlee turned toward an officer—the same one she had nodded to when the bike drew beside his patrol unit. Concern—and maybe shock—filled his eyes.

"Y …yeah, I'm okay," Charlee stammered. Blood dripped from her forehead onto her cheek.

"How did you do it, kid?" the officer asked. "How'd you ride so fast? How'd you stop them? How? I've never seen anything like it." His words were garbled like listening to someone speak underwater.

Charlee's head swirled. She was going to pass out but couldn't let it happen here. They would take her to the hospital. There would be too many questions. The truth was…she didn't know how to answer the questions. She had to get away. Fast. "Bike, go!" Before the officer could ask anything else, the bike sped away with Charlee barely holding on to the handlebars.

"Wait!" the officer called. "You need medical attention."

The words trailed off as the bike jetted away from the financial district.

Skyscrapers shrunk from view. Charlee's aches and pains eased…as if being on the bike helped somehow. But she was still ready to go home. It was enough for one night. The bike must have agreed. Neighborhoods filled with businesses turned into streets lined by homes. She passed her school and a familiar park. They turned onto her block and then reached home.

In the driveway, she stiffly climbed off the bike and pushed it into the garage. She stood and stared at it.

"What are you?" she asked. "Why have you come into my life? Are we meant to do something special together?"

The answers would have to wait. For now, with one last look at the strange two-wheeler, she closed the garage door and went into the house. Charlee painfully cleaned the spilled soda from earlier then grabbed another bottle and finished half of it. After half walking, half crawling up the stairs to her bedroom, she crashed into bed and passed out.

Then the dream returned.

Chapter 11

The Castle, the Princess, and the Giant

Charlee stood at the start of a cobblestone path lined by trees with branches stripped of nearly all their leaves. Those that remained were gray and lifeless, hanging limp from dried branches. Charlee listened for the tiny whispers of the leaf creatures, but they were silent. Overhead the emerald sky was darkening, and in the distance heavy storm clouds covered the land in shadows. Thunder boomed over her shoulder.

At the end of the cobblestone path stood a great wall. It had to be the one she had seen from afar in her last dream.

"I must be at the other end of the valley," she reasoned, turning away from the path and staring at the mountain range where she had most likely stood before. "But something's wrong." The land should have been covered in blue grass, but the fields were withered and dried. Charlee shivered as the sky cracked with another explosion. Again she listened for any sounds of life. Nothing!

"I don't like this. Why do I keep returning to this world? Why do these dreams seem so real?"

She wore the same scratchy clothing and long boots as before with the sword at her side. If this dream played out like the first two, she would soon see the woman whose song was so sad and the giant man determined to hurt her.

With cautious steps, Charlee walked along the path toward the wall. It loomed larger with each stride. The wall was built from white grainy stones marked by crystalline spots glistening under an orange sun the storm would soon swallow. Each stone was about the size of a minivan and they were stacked ten stories high.

Charlee stopped when she reached an open archway that towered over her for what seemed like miles, guarded on either side by statues hewn into the stone wall. She gazed at the statues, knights in armor, one male, the other female, each holding a sword to their chest.

Fear urged that she turn back. Curiosity proved stronger. "Let's see what happens." She slipped through the entryway and entered into a city stretched out in either direction. It was a city built under the shadows of a mountain range. A glimmering white castle chiseled into the side of the largest mountain stood like a watchful protector. A waterfall fell from a peak above the castle and disappeared within its walls.

Charlee marveled at the city. Each structure built without disturbing nature appeared made of organic elements. Giant trees served as skyscrapers. Boulders, some as large as four-story buildings, had been hewn into what might have been shops where vendors sold their wares. Roads paved with the same white stone as the great wall wound throughout this city, but it appeared that no tree, no plant, no field, nor a single blade of grass had been uprooted to build this city.

But where were the people? This strange city was empty. The shops built into boulders appeared open but without the vendors and shoppers.

"This can't be good." Charlee took a few steps forward and listened. Besides the waterfall, she was alone. "Hello, is there anyone here?" More silence, except for distant thunder. "Yes, I must be losing it to have such dreams."

"Losing what?" The gentle, musical voice made Charlee turn. There stood the woman with golden hair. Her white dress shimmered as it captured what remained of the sunlight. Her crystal blue eyes probed Charlee as if assessing whether she was friend or enemy.

"Where did you come from? You weren't here a second ago," Charlee pointed out in the women's Lengoron language.

"But I was," the woman countered as thunder rumbled this time much louder and closer. The storm succeeded in blocking the sun, casting a chilly shade over the city. A gust of wind swept down from the sky and brushed against Charlee's face. Was this the dream's way of hinting danger approached?

Charlee shrunk away. "Look, it's nice to see you, but I have to be going. I have to wake up from this dream now."

"You speak strange words." A smile danced across the woman's face. "But never mind that, young knight. You have returned home."

"Home?"

"Why, yes. Doesn't this feel like home?" Lightning flashed for the first time followed by thunder as loud as any monsoon summer storm she had ever experienced. It rattled the ground.

"No…well, maybe." Charlee remembered that Saur had said something similar. She gazed around the city. Though she wanted to run away from a sense of dread that tied her stomach in knots, this place was familiar. *But why?* This was a fantasy her mind had created, nothing more. Maybe that's why it felt familiar. She made this dream world, so of course she would feel a connection—right?

"Will you trust me, young knight?" The woman stepped closer.

"Uh, yeah." Charlee puzzled over that question. *Why shouldn't I trust her?* "Can I ask your name?"

"Why, of course, young knight. I am Princess Theodora." More lightning—more thunder followed the announcement of her name.

Charlee flinched at the flash overhead then chuckled. "A princess—these are strange dreams—I've never ever had dreams about a princess in a fairy-tale land. But I guess there's a first for everything."

"Again, your words are strange, but I sense goodness in your heart. By what name are you known?"

"I'm…Charlee."

"Well, Char…Lee, it is fine to meet a brave young knight such as yourself." Theodora bowed deeply. "As I mentioned in our last encounter, I have not often met a lady knight, but I do know they are every bit the knights that men are. May I ask you another question?"

"Sure."

"Has a quest caused you to return here?"

"A quest?"

"Yes." The smile disappeared from Theodora's face. "I mean, have you promised an oath to anyone? Are you on a quest that only the bravest knight might dare?"

"Uh, no. I haven't promised an oath to anyone, and I'm not on a quest. At least, not as far as I know."

Lightning struck in the field just outside the city's wall. Theodora fell to her knees. Tears welled up in her eyes. "Then would you swear an oath to me?"

"What?"

"Forgive me, brave Char…Lee, but I find myself without a knight, and I am so very frightened."

"I don't get it." Charlee placed a hand on Theodora's shoulder then quickly recoiled. Her fingers froze as if she had just touched ice.

"I am in danger. There is an evil knight, the one called Tribon, who serves the empress. You have challenged him once before beside the water. Char…Lee, brave knight, the empress has sworn to kill me because I am of royal blood. She has sent Tribon to end my life. I am afraid that I will die unless I have the protection of one such as yourself. I could pay you well."

"You…you want me to help you?" Charlee stepped back as yet another streak of lightning and crash of thunder filled the sky. "Isn't there anyone else…maybe someone a bit bigger than me? Where are all the people?"

"The conjurers are gone, taken by the empress. She feeds on their spirits. The non-magics have been enslaved."

Charlee fingered the handle of the sword at her side. What was this princess talking about? An evil knight and an empress! Then again, since this was a dream, Charlee could do anything she wanted…even battle a giant knight. *I can be the hero.* "I…I will help you."

A smile glowed on Princess Theodora's face. The tears disappeared. The sky above started to clear. "Oh, thank you. I shall forever be indebted to you." Theodora wrapped long, thin arms around Charlee. A chill froze the air moving in and out of her lungs, making it hard to breathe.

When the embrace ended, Charlee inhaled as deeply as she could. She took a few breaths before she could speak. "So, uh, I guess I should get you to a safe place somewhere."

"Alas, I fear there is no safe place where I can hide—at least, not in this world."

"What do you mean?"

"Young knight, you have a power that you are not aware of." Princess Theodora circled Charlee.

"Huh?"

"You possess the power to open a gateway to another world—a world where I could be safe from Tribon and the empress—a world where they could never harm me."

"Huh?" Charlee followed Theodora with her eyes.

"Young knight, you want to protect me, don't you?"

"Yeah."

"Then use your power. Open the gateway and let me pass through. We have not a moment to waste." Theodora stared with those crystal eyes, so innocent and afraid, yet so determined.

"I'm sorry." Charlee bowed her head. "I don't know what power you're talking about. I'm not the person you think I am."

"I know exactly who you are." Theodora's voice grew desperate—almost angry. "You are the keeper of the gateway. You only need to look into yourself to know the truth. You must try! I fear that Tribon will be upon us soon."

Charlee paced in front of Theodora—hands on her head. "How do I open this gateway?"

"You need only use your mind."

"Are you joking? I'm just a normal girl, you know. I'm not really a knight. Maybe it's time for me to wake up now."

"Young knight, you must believe in yourself as I believe in you. Just close your eyes and think of a world you know—a world you care for—and you will be able to open a gateway to that world. You can do it. Concentrate!"

Charlee sighed and closed her eyes. She would give it a try. She thought of home—Mom, Megan, even Dad. Then the thoughts wandered to school, and to one particular student—Sandra. The images shifted to her neighborhood and the great skyscrapers of San Francisco. She peered down at the city as if from a cloud. Picture after picture flooded her mind, one morphing into another.

"Good, young knight! You're doing it!"

Theodora's voice made Charlee's eyes open. A ball of blue light had formed and hovered in the air just above the ground. It grew into a swirling, dazzling blue vortex. Earth hovered in the vortex. Theodora stepped into the light as if to cross over to…Earth. Of course, it was all just a dream.

"No!"

Charlee grew rigid at the gruff voice behind her. It was the massive knight, Tribon. She twisted just as the knight with the red beard rushed through the archway in the great wall on the largest horse she had ever seen.

"Young knight, do not let him into the gateway!" Theodora cried. "He will kill me!" The princess began to vanish in the blue light. "Remember, young knight. You swore to protect me." The faint whisper of Theodora's words remained in Charlee's mind as the princess disappeared from sight.

Charlee wasn't about to let Tribon get to Theodora. Since this was only a dream, she would fight and kill the giant knight if necessary. Charlee concentrated on closing the gateway before Tribon could follow. It worked. The blue energy faded until it had shrunk to the size of a marble. Then it popped out of existence.

Tribon jumped from the horse, unsheathed his massive sword in one smooth motion, and then rushed at Charlee.

Maybe fighting this giant knight isn't such a good idea. Maybe it would be better to run. She turned to flee, only to stumble and fall onto the stone roadway. Tribon, steam rising from his nostrils, eyes wild, stood over her.

She was done for. *Good thing it's only a dream.*

Then, Tribon knelt until his face was just a few feet above her. He opened his mouth revealing yellow, broken teeth. Deep lines etched into his leathery skin, and strands of white wove through his bushy red beard. When he lifted his face again, regret seemed to replace the anger. Or maybe it was… disappointment.

"What have you done, young one?" Tribon asked gravely, shaking his head. The knight then faded away like an apparition.

Charlee was left alone, but the echo of Tribon's words hung in the air. *What have you done, young one?*

Chapter 12

The Next Day

Charlee woke up this morning with broken glasses in her pajama pocket, a bruised forehead that looked like it had been healing for days, and a body that ached all over. It could all easily be explained. She could have fallen out of bed, bumped her head, and just didn't remember. That had to be it because none of that craziness with the bike happened, right?

"I mean, where did all my powers go?" She needed glasses again to see and had to rely on an old pair to replace the ones that broke during the night. Charlee touched her bicep. It felt squishy—no sign of any super strength. The hearing that had led her to the burglar had also disappeared. Yes, it had all been a strange dream—every bit of it from the bike to the superpowers to the fairytale land with a princess and evil knight.

That made sense, except for the report on the morning news Charlee overheard on the kitchen television. The reporter told of a mysterious kid on a bike doing some heroic acts last night that sounded just like her dreams.

Before leaving for school, her parents had wanted to talk, but she avoided them. After replacing her broken glasses and catching the morning news story, she ran out the door toward school convinced the report was just a coincidence.

Charlee staggered onto the Myron Applebee school grounds, head heavy as the night's event swirled into questions of reality versus dreams. "They're just so real. Am I starting to lose my mind? Am I flipping out because I can't handle San Francisco? Is Tina Lomeli getting to me?" she tried to reason out at her locker. "I have to get a grip."

"Hey, you!" Sandra appeared from behind a group of students.

Charlee, dressed in a purple hooded sweatshirt, placed the hood over her head. *What am I doing—trying to disguise myself? Stupid.*

"Why are you wearing a hood?" Sandra frowned. "Is that allowed?"

Charlee hadn't thought of that. "I guess not." She removed the hood.

"Oh my God!" Sandra clenched her fists.

"What?"

"Where'd you get that scratch on your head? And what's with the old, funky glasses? Did Tina have anything to do with it? I'll bust her lip open."

"It wasn't Tina."

"Did you crash on your bike? You didn't damage that cool bike, did you? I'd never forgive you."

"Uh, yeah, I fell on the bike. But don't worry…the bike's fine. I'm fine, too, by the way—in case you were wondering."

Sandra chuckled as the bell for first period sounded. "See you in math," she said. "Then we'll do lunch. Don't get in line at the cafeteria. I made you a tuna and peanut butter sandwich. Sound good?"

"Huh?" Charlee shrugged.

"Kidding…or am I."

§ § §

Charlee stared at the algebra quiz. On any other day, a math quiz would be a breeze, but not today. Too much clouded her mind. Beside her Sandra's hand moved quickly through each formula. Examining the quiz sheet, the equations seemed to dance together.

Come on. Focus.

She just couldn't. Dreams danced across her mind. The last words Tribon spoke before fading away hung in Charlee's thoughts. But if they were only a bunch of crazy dreams what did any of this matter? It didn't. *Get back to the quiz.*

At that moment, for some unexplainable reason, Charlee glanced up toward the classroom window. *No!* She nearly jumped from the chair. There, standing outside—bent over and peering through the window—was the giant knight. *Tribon!*

Charlee gasped. It couldn't be. Weary eyes had to be playing a trick. Or she had fallen asleep. *Wake up! Wake up, now!* She looked again. He still stood there, his dark eyes squared on her. There was no mistaking the mane of red hair that surrounded his face and the graying beard. His features were burnt into her memory.

No, it was just a dream! He wasn't really there! Charlee covered her eyes with the quiz. *Please don't be there.* When she removed the paper, Tribon had disappeared. *I am losing my mind for sure.* Heart crashing like waves battering a cliff, she once again eyed Sandra, who stared back as if to ask, *"What is it?"*

Charlee nodded in a gesture to show all was fine, but it wasn't. Something was definitely wrong. When she turned back to the window, a massive handprint covered much of the glass.

Her hands shook and face grew flushed even as a cold sweat formed. *I have to know.* She slowly rose and walked up to the math teacher. "Mrs. Billerby, I'm not feeling well." Charlee's voice was hushed and quivered. "I think I'm going to be sick."

"Yes, Charlee, you look pale," Mrs. Billerby said. "Don't worry about the quiz. You can finish it tomorrow."

"Thank you." Charlee walked slowly toward the classroom door. Hesitating before opening it she took a deep breath, twisted the doorknob, and gently cracked the door. A peek into the hallway revealed no Tribon. With classes in session, the campus remained quiet. Charlee laughed silently.

"I didn't really see Tribon. It's just that the dream is on my mind…that's all. It's making me see things," she whispered.

She wanted to believe that. It made sense. Not convinced, she slipped down the hallway, careful to avoid the view of Mrs. Billerby or any other teacher who might see through classroom windows. "What am I doing?" she said out loud, launching a search through the school for the giant knight.

Charlee moved stealthily from hallway to hallway. Around every corner, behind rows of lockers, she tensed at what might be hidden on the other side. Her search uncovered nothing. Tribon wasn't there.

"Stop it! Just stop this, now!" she commanded herself. "Look what you're doing to yourself. And all over some dreams."

Ready to go back to class, something flashed at the far end of the soccer field. Something…shiny. It glimmered under the late morning sunlight. No telling what it was. But it shouldn't have been there. "Don't go. Return to class. Finish your quiz. Get on with your normal life."

Charlee didn't listen to herself. Instead, she made the long trek to the soccer field. As she neared the object, her legs wobbled and she shivered. A large sword had been thrust into the ground. The sun danced across the long blade's mirror-like smoothness.

"Run!" Charlee mouthed, starting to back up.

"Running will do you no good."

Chapter 13

Face To Face With a Giant

Charlee felt her knees buckle. "It can't be!"

She whirled around to face the giant knight who haunted her dreams. "It's him, but how! It was just a dream. Not real. I must still be dreaming. Wake up!" She pinched herself on the arm, but the knight remained.

He wore a long, dark robe with a thick black belt around his waist. Two curved daggers with spiraling handles made of what looked like green snakeskin hung from the belt. A red sash wrapped around a shoulder, across his chest and stretched to his hip. Attached to it was an ornately carved long and narrow wooden sheath for the sword.

Charlee closed her eyes, hoping that when she opened them again the knight would be gone, but it didn't work. "I'm losing my mind right in the middle of school," she decided as she turned to go back to her classroom.

"There's no point in running." The knight articulated each word.

"I'm not going to run."

"I can see in your eyes that you are contemplating an escape, but I assure you it is not worth the effort. I will appear to you no matter where you go. You see, I'm not really here. I'm in your mind, so to speak."

"So I really am losing my mind."

"You speak foolish words." Tribon's voice was harsh. "I would expect more from the one chosen to save the world...or maybe two worlds."

What did he say? "I don't understand," she said warily.

"You will." This time, the giant knight softened his voice.

Charlee backpedaled from the knight. "Look, all I know is that you're some evil dude from my dreams. So if you're here and I'm awake, something is wrong."

Tribon took one large step and closed the distance between him and Charlee. "I am not your enemy, young knight, but you and this world are in danger. You must prepare yourself. This is more than a dream."

"Good to know."

Tribon moved to the sword in the ground and ripped it free. He cleaned it with a gloved hand before sliding it into its sheath. "I am Tribon. Though I believe you are already aware of my name, you do not know the truth of who I am. I was a general sworn to protect Latara, one of the Ten Unified Kingdoms of a world called Janasara. I served at the side of Michala, the Guardian. After his defeat at the Battle of Latara, I vowed I would spend the rest of my life trying to destroy Empress Theodora, who rules over all of Janasara with her dark magic."

Charlee stopped her slow retreat. "Wait! You're the one who serves an evil empress. Theodora was the good princess trying to get away from the empress…and you."

Tribon sighed and looked to the school grounds. "I think it best if we move to a more suitable location to talk. Though I cannot be seen by any but you, prying eyes might think your current actions strange."

"I don't get it. What did you say earlier? You're in my mind?"

"Please, allow us to carry on behind that structure." Tribon pointed to a trailer at the edge of the field used as a temporary classroom. It was not in use this period. "Please, I mean you no harm. I am here to help."

Charlee reluctantly agreed and followed Tribon to the backside of the trailer. *What am I doing? Just run, fool!* But she didn't. Maybe it was the urgency in Tribon's voice, but suddenly he didn't seem like someone she should fear. Not that any of this was real.

"You have been the victim of Theodora's trickery, young one." Tribon lowered to one knee as Charlee joined him at the trailer. He still towered over her. "You see, we once lived in peace in a time when evil had been destroyed and good magic was used to foster prosperity. Conjurers and non-magics lived side by side in every community. But then Theodora became a mistress of the dark arts and rose to power. She brought evil back to Janasara. She destroyed the conjurers to feed her dark powers, and then enslaved the non-magics. Now my world lives under her vicious rule. No, Theodora is no princess. She is indeed a vile, ruthless empress." His words flowed quickly and in English rather than the language of her dreams.

Charlee cleared her throat. "How are…I mean, how do you know English?"

"I have learned your language through your mind," Tribon answered.

"Okay. Well, I've got to be going now, but, hey, it was nice meeting you."

"Stay, there is more to tell. It was foretold by the Ancient Scrolls that there would someday come a guardian—the Last Guardian—a young knight who would rise up in a dark hour when the light of a guardian was the only hope. This is that hour and I believe you to be that guardian."

Charlee gulped.

Tribon lowered his head. "I just never thought the Last Guardian would be a short, round girl so untested in battle."

"Huh?"

"You do not yet fully understand the terrible force you have unleashed on this world...I believe you call it Earth."

"I don't know what you're talking about," Charlee snapped. "And I really have to be going to class now."

Tribon continued as if he had not heard her. "I take blame for the ease with which Theodora used you to enter this world. I should have done more to stop you. Maybe I should have struck you down. She had you under her spell, clouding your vision. Theodora's power is that strong."

Charlee's head ached from information overload. "I don't understand a word you're saying."

"Then try to understand this," the knight said gravely. "Using the power of dreams, Theodora reached out across the great divide between the worlds, and she found you. I don't know how, but she found you. She invaded your mind and used your power to make you open a gateway—a portal separating worlds—so that she could physically enter Earth."

Tribon grasped his sword's handle. "You were the only one who had the key to open the gateway because only the guardians possess such a power. For generations the guardians wielded their power as a bridge between the kingdoms, to unite them against evil wherever it arose. But one guardian, Michala, discovered the great divide. Only he had the power to create a bridge between worlds. You, young knight, come from Michala's bloodline. You have his power. Theodora knew this and exploited you."

Taking a long breath, Tribon continued, "Young knight, you are the Last Guardian. You must understand this, or all is lost. You must stop Theodora and correct the mistake you made in allowing her to reach Earth. Otherwise, your world will face the same fate as Janasara."

"But that only happened in a dream." Charlee leaned against the trailer. She wanted to slump to the ground but didn't want to appear so weak, even if this was a dream.

"When it comes to magic," Tribon explained, "there is no barrier between the physical reality and the dream reality. Theodora made you a pawn. She used the shadowy layer of dreams to have you open the gateway, and in Janasara that gateway became real. Make no mistake, she is here...now."

Charlee rubbed her head. "But why would she want to come here?"

"Michala stole something of great value from Theodora," Tribon rose to his feet. "Just before the battle in which he fell, he stole her immortality. She believes that he opened a portal into this world and hid it here. She believes as I that since you share his power, his spirit dwells within you—and thus you know where her immortality is."

"What? That doesn't make any sense." Charlee pushed away from the trailer and moved to within a foot of the knight. She fought the urge to jump up and snag his beard, but he had said he wasn't really here—that he was just a spirit. "How did this Michala person steal her immortality? And how am I supposed to know where it is?"

Tribon backed up. Perhaps it was because with Charlee standing so close, he couldn't see her beneath his bushy beard. "Theodora's immortality is carried in a medallion—a foul creation forged by evil itself in the dark days of long ago," he revealed. "The medallion had been lost in time, its existence thought to be a myth. However, ancient conjurers told stories of its infinite power and ability to grant eternal life. Theodora found this medallion or maybe it found her. She used it to usher in a new dark age. Then Michala stole it. While Theodora's magic is still powerful, without the medallion she is mortal like the rest of us. Without it, she will die, like the rest of us. Already she grows old."

"I don't get it. Theodora's young, beautiful."

"That image was not her true self. Soon enough, you will see Theodora for what she truly is. She will find you. She may have already found you. When you opened the gateway, what did you see when you looked inside the light?"

Charlee quickly reconstructed the dream in her mind. "I saw my family."

"Then she has seen them, as well."

Tribon didn't need to say more. This might not be real, but if her family was in danger she couldn't ignore the warning. If she had somehow opened a portal than her family and everyone else was at risk from Theodora because of her mistake.

"This just doesn't feel like a dream," Charlee said softly. "I've done something very wrong, and I have to fix it." She fought back tears. "What do I do, Tribon? I don't know where the medallion is. I'm not the Last Guardian. I'm just a girl with my own problems."

"It is time to grow up, young knight. Accept who you are. If you want to save Earth, find the medallion. It is your only hope. Use its power against Theodora. Without it, you will be unable to face her, and she will destroy this world as she has Janasara."

"Tribon, I need your help."

The knight lifted one of the daggers in his belt and twirled it between his fingers. Underneath his beard and mustache, his upper lip seemed to rise as if in a slight smile. "I will as much as I can. I said before that only you can see me. I am here only in your mind. I continue to exist in my world, but you have transported my spirit across the great divide. A part of you—a part deep inside you—knows that what I'm saying is true. It is that part that sought my counsel."

"Well, if I goofed and let Theodora across this great divide, can't I open the gateway for you, too?"

"I wish it were so. When a guardian opens a gateway, their power is drained. Now, it will take some time before you will be able to do so again. It will be another rising of the sun, maybe longer, before your power returns and you can safely open another."

"Just great. What am I supposed to do till then?"

"The best you can. You can contact me anytime you need. My spirit will always be at your side."

Charlee turned away from Tribon. She could no longer fight back the tears. They ran down her cheeks. She couldn't cry in front of him. He believed her to be some sort of guardian. But she wasn't. None of this could be true.

It's all in my head, but what if it's true? What if my family is in danger? What am I supposed to do? I can't face some crazy witch from another world. I'm just...me. Then she remembered something that helped—something that just might make it possible to face Theodora. The bike! If Tribon and Theodora were real, perhaps the bike's powers were real, too.

She swung toward the knight. "Tribon—"

"Who's Tribon? Who are you talking to?" Sandra's words unexpectedly came from the field. Sandra walked up to the trailer and stopped just a few feet away, one eyebrow lifted.

Charlee wasn't sure how to introduce Sandra to Tribon, but as it turned out she didn't have to. The knight had vanished. "I'm...talking to myself, who else?"

"You call yourself Tribon?" Sandra asked.

"Well, actually—"

"Charlee Smelton, there you are! I've been looking all over for you." Mrs. Myers, the school principal, approached. "Your mother just contacted the school. Something has happened at the university. Your father's been hurt. He's in the hospital."

"What?" Charlee pulled her cell phone from her pant pocket. A blinking red light indicated someone had just called. It had to be Mom. *Oh, no! It's starting!*

Chapter 14

Facing the Truth

Charlee sat in the passenger seat of Mrs. Zarabe's car, eyes focused ahead on the approaching Cityside Medical Center. The school counselor offered to drive her to the hospital shortly after Principal Myers reported her dad had been hurt. Sandra sat in the backseat. Despite Zarabe's protests, Sandra declared she had to be there for Charlee.

As soon as the car stopped, Charlee threw open the car door and ran inside with Sandra quickly following. At the front counter, an elderly woman offered them a smile. "Can I help you?"

"My dad was hurt." Charlee stuttered as she rushed the words. "They brought him here. Where is he?"

"Sweetie, calm down and tell me his name."

"Joseph Smelton."

Charlee's feet tapped the ground as the woman typed the information into a computer. "Hon, your father's in the intensive care unit. He was taken there from the emergency room an hour ago."

"Where is that?"

"Take the elevator to the third floor, head down the corridor and turn ri…"

Charlee didn't wait. She sprinted to the elevator and anxiously hit the "up" button. *Come on, hurry up!* Repeatedly banging on the button, thoughts of her dad lying hurt in the ICU brought tears. Sandra placed an arm around her shoulder. It was comforting to have Sandra there, even if they had only been friends for a couple of days.

Finally…ping! The elevator arrived. As the door swished open, she rushed in and punched the button for the third floor. When the elevator arrived and the doors opened, she raced to the ICU's towering glass double doors. Charlee hesitated for just a couple of breaths. She couldn't bring herself to step through the doorway.

"It's all right," Sandra offered.

Charlee nodded, pushed through the glass doors and entered a scary world she had never seen—the inside of the Intensive Care Unit. Rooms lined both sides of the corridor, each one filled with patients. Most patients had tubes attached to them. Machines beeped in the background.

Charlee stopped at a counter where a group of nurses was gathered. "I'm looking for my dad…Professor Smelton."

One of the nurses leaned over the counter. "He's in Room 304, straight down this hallway."

This time, Charlee didn't run. Shaky legs tread cautiously but it didn't take long before she stood at the doorway of Room 304. Pressing both hands against the heavy wooden door, she closed her eyes. Blowing out a lungful of air, she pushed the door open and entered. Sandra remained behind.

Charlee's heart immediately sank. Her dad lay on the bed, his head bandaged so only one eye was visible. Tubes in his nose helped him breathe while more tubes were attached to his wrists. A monitor on the wall, which showed his vitals, beeped rhythmically. That had to be a good sign. Her mom stood beside the bed, her face puffy and red as if she had been crying.

"Mom, what happened?" They hugged before her mom spoke. The hug lasted several minutes. It wasn't until then that Charlee realized how much she needed to be enveloped in someone's arms, but she couldn't linger in the moment. Charlee gently pulled away from her mom.

"They said an intruder broke into his office at the university." Her mom blinked away fresh tears. "Your father walked in on him and I guess tried to stop him."

"Will he be okay?"

"The doctors think so. The doctor in the emergency room said he had a concussion and broken ribs." Her voice waivered. "They said the next twenty-four hours…well, they need to watch him closely."

"Did he speak?" Charlee hoped the answer was yes. "Did he say anything about who did this?"

"No. He was unconscious when they brought him in."

Charlee thought for a minute. "Where's Megan?"

"She's with…a friend. I didn't want her to be scared."

Friend? What friend? Charlee didn't verbalize the question. Instead, she hugged her mom tightly one more time, then released her and backed away. The truth took shape. *Theodora is responsible. That means I am responsible, because I allowed her through the gateway.*

Her mom motioned Charlee closer to the bed. "It's all right, sweetheart. Come talk to him. He will hear you."

"Sorry, Mom. I can't stay. There's something I have to do." Charlee started to back out of the room.

Her mother reached a hand out toward her. "Charlee, I know you're going through something right now. Stay with the family, and we can face it together. We are stronger if we stand together."

"Not this time, Mom." Charlee burst out of the room, stopped momentarily to make eye contact with Sandra, and together they ran down the hallway to the elevators. *This was her fault! She had to fix this. I have to find Theodora and stop her before she hurts anyone else.*

§ § §

Back in Mrs. Zarabe's car, Charlee sat quietly as the counselor drove her home. Sandra, who still refused to return to school, also remained quiet in the backseat. Mrs. Zarabe broke the silence. "Now, Charlee, I sure wish you would tell me why you asked me to bring you home. I think you belong back at the hospital with your family. I'd be happy to turn around and drive you back."

Charlee answered with a lie. "Mrs. Zarabe, my mom asked me to pick up some of my dad's stuff."

"I understand." Mrs. Zarabe nodded. "Well, I'll wait for you outside. As soon as you have everything you need, I'll drive you back to the hospital, and Sandra...you will return to school with me—no more arguing."

As they neared the house, Charlee gasped at a crowd of neighbors who had gathered. *Oh no!*

"Oh my stars!" Mrs. Zarabe placed a hand to her mouth. "What is going on here?"

Charlee stared at the huge hole where the front door to the house had been. Shattered charred wood and broken glass lay strewn over the steps leading up to the doorway.

Theodora!

Charlee exited the car and moved past the neighbors. Some whispered to each other whether they should call the police or fire departments. Others asked if anyone had seen what happened. One woman said she had checked the house and no one was inside.

Ignoring their comments and stares, Charlee carefully climbed the splintered steps to the blackened doorway. The damage went farther than the entrance. Theodora had moved through the house, smashing walls, ripping doors off their hinges, flipping couches and chairs over and tearing through

71

drawers. The destruction continued upstairs with chests turned over, walls blackened with burn holes and bathroom mirrors shattered.

A family picture lay on the floor in her parents' bedroom. The glass frame was cracked. Charlee shuddered. Theodora must have gone to the house and found nothing—and, luckily, no one. Something she found then led the sorceress to her dad's office. What had her dad faced? He could have been killed. She placed the family picture on a table. Her jaw tightened.

"I'll find Theodora, and she'll pay!"

"Charlee look at this!" Charlee whirled around. Sandra had slipped from her side and called from another room. Her room! Down the hall, her room revealed a message scrawled on her bedroom mirror. The message, scribed in what looked like blood:

Child, when the Queen of the Night reaches her fullest glory, meet me at the Great Tower that bears a crown. If you do not heed my invitation, your family and everyone you cherish—this entire world—will suffer. Underneath those words was another message in smaller letters. *Recognize this blood. It is your father's. Shall we spill more?*

Searing heat flowed from Charlee's face, burning away tears. She hunched over, sure she would puke, but only dry heaves came. "What have I done!" she said as her body shook. Eying a flashlight on her nightstand, she reached for it and flung it at the mirror, screaming. The glass shattered into tiny shards that littered the floor.

"What's going on, Charlee?" Sandra placed an arm around her shoulder. "Who wrote that on the mirror? What kind of trouble are you in?"

Charlee had forgotten Sandra was still there. "You shouldn't be here."

"Maybe, but I'm here anyway. Tell me what's going on."

"Sandra."

"Charlee."

"I'll tell you, but not here. Let's go." Charlee grabbed Sandra and they ran downstairs, past Mrs. Zarabe and a few neighbors who had entered the house. They didn't stop until they climbed down the steps into the garage. There, Charlee stared wide-eyed at the ruins of what had been their garage. Scattered tools and splintered timber covered the floor. Beams from the ceiling had collapsed, bringing down a small section of roof.

"Where's my bike? Please be here!" She searched through the rubble.

Something rattled under a mound of rubble and dirty clothes in a corner. Charlee took a few steps back, dragging Sandra with her. The rattling intensified until…the bike performed a wheelie and jumped from the pile.

"Bike! Yes!" Charlee embraced the ugly two-wheeler. The bike seemed unharmed. At least, if it had any new scratches, she couldn't tell them apart from old ones. "Bike, I'm in trouble. I need you."

As soon as she touched the handlebars, a wave of calm—a wave of strength—a wave of certainty flowed into her. "Wait a second! If Theodora didn't take you or destroy you, it must mean she doesn't know about you." That meant she had one surprise. Maybe she could face Theodora after all. But first she had to get the bike out of the garage.

The heavy garage door hung off its hinges, blocking the exit. Charlee let go of the bike, went to the hulk that had been the garage door and rammed it with her shoulder. The huge door broke free and flew down the driveway, barely missing the bystanders still gathered around the house.

"How'd you do that?" Sandra asked.

"Come on," Charlee motioned for Sandra to hop on the bike. Truth was, Charlee wasn't sure how she gained such strength, but it had something to do with the bike. She didn't know how or why the bike gave her powers, but now was not the time to ask.

They both climbed onto the seat, still ignoring stares from Mrs. Zarabe and the gawkers from the neighborhood. "Hold on tight," Charlee urged, peering back at Sandra. The bike wasted no time. It zipped down the driveway, into the street and, like a blur, blasted away from the destruction.

Sandra clutched Charlee's waist. "What's happening?"

As they rode, the streets grew fuzzy. With one hand on the handlebars, Charlee lifted the glasses from her face and the world became clear, every detail sharp, like seeing the entire city through a telescope.

With the powers the bike granted her, Charlee scanned the city streets for any signs of Theodora. The burning in her face spread throughout her body. She couldn't think, couldn't feel anything but rage. She had to find Theodora fast. The witch hurt her father, threatened the rest of her family, and destroyed their home. One word plagued her mind. *Revenge!*

"Charlee," Sandra coughed as she tried to speak over the wind rushing past the speeding bike, "I know you're hurting, but you have to think about what you're doing. This woman is messing with your head. Don't let her. You'll lose."

Sandra's words cut through Charlee's fury. She pulled back on the handlebars, directing the bike to slow, even as every ounce of her being wanted to face Theodora and make her pay for every hurt she caused. "So what should I do?"

Sandra leaned toward Charlee's ear. "We plan, girl!"

Chapter 15

Spilling It All

"Y ou have to tell me everything." Sandra sat down crossed-legged on her bedroom floor and motioned for Charlee to do the same.

Sandra's room was comfortable. A violin rested on a stand by her bed. Sheet music was strewn over her desk. Posters of rock bands covered her walls. Pictures of what must have been her mom and dad and maybe an older sister covered a dresser. A few loose T-shirts and jeans littered the floor. Her room was without a mirror—probably by choice. Sandra didn't seem to wear makeup or fuss with her hair. She had her priorities straight—family and music.

"You won't believe me," Charlee muttered.

"How can I not believe you?" Sandra replied. "I've seen your dad, I've seen your house, I saw that horrible message written in blood—your dad's blood—and I just rode on that…that bike."

Charlee took a deep breath. Had she done the right thing in coming to Sandra's home? It had been her friend's idea. They had to talk, and where else could they have gone? But Sandra was getting too involved, and that meant she too could be in danger.

"Well, tell!" Sandra insisted.

"Okay," Charlee conceded.

She flew into the story, relieved to share it. She didn't leave out a single detail, telling of the strange dreams and of Empress Theodora, of a grandfather from a world called Janasara who was some kind of guardian and how, because they were related, she had some power to unlock a gateway between worlds. Charlee explained how the sorceress was after some magical medallion supposedly hidden in this world.

"Theodora tricked me into opening a gateway. I allowed her to reach Earth and this city." Charlee's hands formed fists. "I've put everyone in danger all because I was stupid. The only chance I have of stopping Theodora is that weird bike. It gives me powers every time I touch it. I just don't understand why. And I don't get why it's come into my life now—it can't just be an accident."

Charlee stood and paced the room. "All I know is the bike and I have to find Theodora before she hurts anyone else, but that message she left is a riddle. I don't know what it means...I don't know what's she's talking about."

Sandra stared at her without uttering a word.

"I told you it was unbelievable." Charlee ran fingers through her brown stringy hair and sat once again on the floor.

"Shh!" Sandra urged.

"What?"

"Wait!" Sandra pointed her finger at Charlee and nodded.

"Uhhhh...what are you doing?" Charlee's confusion showed through her wrinkled brow.

"I got it, dummy! It's so simple." Sandra announced.

"I have no idea what you're talking about."

"It's the riddle, stupid. I know what this Theodora person is talking about. I can't believe you can't figure it out."

Charlee was speechless. Sandra wasn't laughing, wasn't questioning the truth of the story. She had accepted it without question. "What do you mean, it's simple?"

"All right, listen." Sandra leaned in closer. "The Queen of the Night has to be the moon. It's the moon that rules the night, right? The time she's at her fullest glory is when the full moon reaches its highest point in the sky. And, of course, that will be about midnight tonight."

"And what about the tower with a crown?"

Sandra's eyes were bright with determination. "I know you haven't lived here that long, but you couldn't have missed the financial district skyscrapers, could you? That must be what Theodora's talking about. The skyscraper that looks like it wears a crown is the old Bank of America building...I think they call it the 555 California Street building now. That's where she'll be—at midnight. That's got to be it."

"Wow! You're good at this."

"Like I said, it's simple."

"Thanks." Charlee wanted to convey a great deal with that one word. Though they had only been friends a short time, Sandra stood by her without question. How was that possible? Sandra didn't need to get mixed up in this mess, yet she had invited Charlee into her home when others would have kicked her aside.

A knock on the door startled both girls. "Sands, is everything all right? I heard you left school to go to the hospital today with a friend."

"It's my dad," Sandra whispered just as the door opened.

Standing at the doorway was a tall man with eyes as dark as Sandra's. He was dressed in slacks, a white shirt, and blue tie. A gun was holstered by his shoulder and a golden badge clipped to his belt. "Is everything all right?" Mr. Flores asked.

"Yes, Dad," Sandra answered. "This is my friend, Charlee. Her dad was hurt today, and I wanted to be there for her."

Mr. Flores glowered at his daughter, started to open his mouth as if to speak, but instead offered a slight smile. "Charlee, it's nice to meet you. Is your father all right?"

"I...I don't know yet," Charlee spoke softly.

"Well, let me know if we can help in any way. Sandra, we will talk about your actions later." With that, Sandra's dad closed the door.

"Uh, is your dad a—"

"He's the deputy police chief, but never mind that right now. We have to decide how we get ready for this Theodora?"

"What do you mean?"

"Well, you clearly can't face her on your own. You need me. So let's get a plan ready for how we're going to take her down and save the world."

Charlee stood. She couldn't allow Sandra to participate anymore. She couldn't endanger her new friend. "You can't go."

"What!" Sandra climbed to her feet.

"I mean it's too dangerous. Thanks for helping me figure things out, but I can't let you go."

"Charlee, you can't do this without me."

"Sure I can. Just because you figured out some riddle doesn't mean I can't face Theodora without the great Sandra. I may have a few tricks up my sleeve, you know."

"What tricks?"

"I don't know, just tricks. It doesn't matter. You can't go."

They paused. A clock ticked on a far wall. Sandra's computer hummed. Mr. Flores cleared his throat somewhere in the house.

Charlee broke the silence between the two of them. "Look, if you go, you could get hurt. I can't let that happen. I...well...I just can't let anyone hurt you. I won't!"

Sandra softened. "Charlee, I can take care of myself."

Charlee rubbed her forehead. The bruise from the night before was nearly gone. "All right, you can go. And you're right—we need to plan. But first, can I use a bathroom?"

"It's down the hall to the left." Sandra's face beamed. "I'll gather some paper, pens, and pencils so we can map out our plan."

"Good idea." Charlee quickly walked out, closing the door behind her. Instead of going to the bathroom, she darted downstairs where she found Sandra's dad. "Uh, Mr. Flores," she whispered.

"Yes?"

"I just thought you should know…Sandra is planning to sneak out tonight. She said something about going to see the skyscrapers. I told her we can't, but she insisted. I don't want to see her get hurt. That's all. Well, sir, I have to go, but I thought you should know." She then slunk to the front door, swung it open and ran outside to her waiting bike. Inside the house, she heard Mr. Flores' booming voice. "Sandra Flores, get down here."

Charlee closed her eyes. Sandra would hate her for this but she had no choice. She had to protect Sandra, and this was the only way to do it. Perhaps Sandra would forgive her…someday. As she rode away, she glanced back at the house. Sandra watched from her bedroom window, eyes filled with anger and hurt. Charlee wished at that moment she didn't have this super vision to see Sandra's face so clearly…but she did.

"Heck, if I save the world, she'll have to forgive me, right? I mean, who could hate a hero?"

Chapter 16

The Great Tower

The 52-story 555 California Street building was still blocks away, but its peak rose high above the financial district's other skyscrapers. Night had long since fallen and the concrete-and-glass giant looked like a ladder to the moon.

Charlee rode for block after block, eyes trained on the sky-touching Goliath. The strange powers the bike granted her had returned. Her legs felt strong as if she could leap over the tallest building. Her hands felt like they could bend steel. None of it prevented the cold rising up her back. As she neared her destination, Charlee's stomach cramped and her heart beat wildly as if horses stampeding inside her chest.

"I should have brought Sandra with me." Charlee lowered her stare to the pavement as she rolled within a block of the California Street building. "She wouldn't be afraid and she'd know what to do. I'm just a scared little girl, not a hero…not some guardian."

The 555 California Street building towered over the city. She had seen the building before, but she never paid attention to the fact that from certain angles, it did look like a crown resting on the rooftop.

"Ride away," she reasoned with herself. "You're not ready for this."

Instead, Charlee climbed off the bike. The moon glowed full and yellow. "How am I going to get into the building at this hour? And how can I reach the roof? There's no way."

She had wanted to be there in the daytime to enter the building, take an elevator to the roof, and hide. But once she left Sandra's, she and the bike stopped a car careening out of control moments before it ran into a park filled with kids. Then they had saved some city workers trapped under the street when a sink hole they were repairing caved in. It seemed at every corner someone needed some kind of help. While it felt good to help, all the heroics had prevented her from reaching her destination sooner.

By the time she had reached the financial district exhaustion began to set in, but when she felt her head droop somehow the bike recharged her. The strength she had used up was restored.

"All right, bi—"

A white mist began to form around the top floors of the skyscraper. It started as a patch of haze circling around the upper levels. At the rooftop, the mist morphed into a thick, gray fog.

"That's not normal. Must be Theodora," Charlee figured.

Late-night inhabitants and visitors to the city streets walked by, and no one seemed to notice the mist enveloping the clear night sky.

"Can no one else see what I'm seeing? But it's right there. Maybe it's for my eyes only."

A faint cry for help reached Charlee's ears. Muffled at first, the plea quickly intensified. Just like the fog, no one else seemed to respond. Maybe they didn't hear it—they didn't have her special sonar-like ears.

"Someone, please!" It was a child's voice coming from the northern side of California Street. Leaving the bike on the sidewalk, Charlee followed the sound across the street, and then around the corner. The cry grew louder with each step.

"Why isn't anyone else coming to help?" Charlee muttered under her breath. "They must be able to hear it by now."

Then the voice stopped. The street was oddly deserted, as if it had been blocked off to traffic and to people. Charlee wondered if the sorceress had supernaturally blocked it off.

"This was a mistake," she muttered as a wind started to blow. At first gentle, it grew forming a howling vortex. *Get out of here!* She ran, but gusts engulfed her. Charlee called out to the bike, but the wind muffled her plea. Swirling faster, the gale lifted her off the pavement and carried her toward the rooftop...*and the meeting with Theodora*, she understood with a sense of grim determination.

Charlee coughed and wheezed as the vortex boxed her in and sucked away the air. She gasped for each shallow breath. *Can't breathe! What do I do?* She placed a hand against her chest to steady herself. Theodora wanted to strike fear. Charlee couldn't give into it. Eyes closed, she concentrated on each breath, knowing she had to stay calm and ready.

"Bike!" she called one more time, but the words couldn't reach the two-wheeler. But what was the point anyway? What could the bike do? Sure it has powers—sure it can jump—but it can't fly. How could it reach her?

Charlee peered up as she neared the top of the building. The fog was thick, blocking any view of the building's upper levels. "Okay, focus!"

The air turned icy as she passed into the barrier. Her vision was cut to just a couple feet in all directions. She grabbed her arms to warm herself. A frosty vapor flowed from her mouth with each word. Evil was nearby. She didn't need the unnaturally frigid air to realize that. "If I show fear, I've already lost."

From somewhere above, Theodora's voice boomed. "I await you, young one."

"This isn't going to be good," Charlee whispered as the wind tunnel that carried her skyward stopped and the gust gave way to a gentle breeze. The fog vanished next. Charlee had arrived at the rooftop. Some unseen force still held her aloft, her dangling legs just inches from the building's edge. The large moon, now visible over her shoulder, shed a yellow glow over the city, but Theodora was nowhere to be seen.

"Theodora, let me go and show yourself!" Charlee demanded.

"I hear hatred in your voice. Why?" asked Theodora's disembodied voice.

"Because I know what you are. I know what you've done." Charlee scanned the roof again. The sorceress' voice echoed from all directions.

"Enlighten me, then." Theodora released Charlee from the magical grip and she dropped hard onto the cement roof.

Hovering above a ledge, the sorceress materialized as the same beautiful young woman from the dreams. Flowing golden hair cast a white glow over the darkness. Crystal blue eyes sparkled.

"I know why you're here." Charlee stood and took a few steps back from the young woman.

Theodora floated to the ground and glided until she was an arm's length from Charlee. With soft, thin fingers, she reached out and stroked her cheek. The ice touch burned just as it had in the dreams.

"You have no reason to fear me," Theodora whispered. "Truly, your hatred of me is unnecessary."

"I know what you want, and I don't have it." Charlee shrunk away from the empress.

Theodora laughed and her eyes turned fiery red. "You say you know what I am. What is it that you know?"

"I know that you used me to open a gateway to cross some great divide. I know that you've come here for a medallion that will let you live forever. You think I have it, but I don't. I can't help you."

"You know nothing." Theodora's cold, deep laugh echoed across the rooftop as her appearance shifted. The young woman grew older. Full cheeks became shallow and bony. Hardened lines etched themselves into an ashen gray face. "Do you know why you were able to open a gateway?"

Charlee ogled the aging sorceress. "It's because I'm a guardian, or something like that."

"Precocious girl, you are right. You are a guardian—the Last Guardian. You are right about something else, too. I have come seeking the medallion that will grant me eternal life. It is rightfully mine. It was stolen from me by a man to whose bloodline you belong. That man was my dear brother-in-law. Do you understand me?"

"What are you saying?"

"Can't you figure it out?" Theodora grasped Charlee's chin. "I would have thought that you were smart enough."

"Just tell me." Charlee shook free of Theodora's grip.

"The man who stole my medallion was married to my sister. They had a child, a daughter, whom they sent to this world. That child was my niece and she is an adult now. You are her daughter and therefore you are my great-niece. Instead of fighting me, you should give your great-aunt a hug."

"I don't believe you!" Charlee looked away from the sorceress. What was it Tribon said? Something about her being part of a bloodline? What did he mean? Could her mother be from another world—from Theodora's world? *It can't be. It just can't be.*

Theodora circled Charlee. "It is of no consequence whether you believe me. Just understand that I will hurt your whole family, as I did your father, if you do not bring me my medallion. Then I will destroy this worthless world you call Earth. Better yet, I will conquer this world and claim it as my own."

"I told you, I don't have your medallion!"

"Then find it!" The sorceress raised her hand as if to strike Charlee but stopped and grinned. Her aging cheeks softened and the wrinkles disappeared as the image of the young blonde princess returned. "I will give you until the queen rises again."

Charlee took a deep breath. "A day! You're giving me a day. Kiss my butt, lady. I'm not going to help you."

"Then I will ravage this world until I find it on my own," Theodora fumed. "Is that what you would have me do—bring utter destruction to everyone and everything you hold dear? Then it is time for you to die. May the last thought in your puny mind be that you have sealed the fate of your family, friends, and this Earth."

Theodora grew in size, towering over Charlee. Clouds formed in the night sky and blocked out the glimmering moon and stars. Lightning blazed. Thunder roared.

Charlee ducked and shielded her eyes from the lightning. When she peeked through fingers, Theodora stood over her, arms raised as she uttered strange words.

Hallat Trissa Meya Nessimarta Lussara!

It was Lengoron, and Charlee understood every word. *Fire Fill My Hands.* It had to be a dark incantation. A crimson glow surrounded Theodora's hands.

Charlee sprinted toward a ledge.

"You cannot run." Theodora's words filled her head, eclipsing all thought.

Light flashed behind Charlee as she dived to the ground. A fiery bolt of energy shot past and struck the ledge just a few feet ahead, blasting a hole through the cement. Charlee rose to her knees. Theodora's laughter rumbled louder than the thunder. Flames shot from Theodora's eyes. The beautiful maiden morphed as thin and gray hair flew wildly around a withered face. Theodora's body lost all form, more spirit than person.

Charlee inched over to the ledge and peered over the edge. It was a long way down. There was no escape.

"Child, prepare to die!"

She wasn't ready to give up. Theodora couldn't win, not this easily. Not on this roof. "Bike! If you can hear me, I need help!"

"Such a waste!" Theodora's voice softened. "As my great-niece, you could have joined me. You could have learned from me. You could have had everything your heart desires. I will mourn what could have been between us."

Theodora again uttered the incantation, bringing fourth more of the deadly energy. Charlee clenched her teeth and waited for the blow, but it never came. A cry ripped through the darkness as a winged creature swooped down and circled the roof. Then it landed in front of the sorceress. Charlee blinked. *What?* She blinked again and rubbed her eyes. The bike stood before her, long, feathered white wings spread out on either side of the frame. It wasn't alone. Sandra sat in the banana seat, hands locked on the handlebars.

"Sandra?"

"Hurry! Get on!" Charlee grabbed Sandra's hand and jumped onto the back of the banana seat. The bike jetted off into the sky with one powerful thrust of its wings. But they weren't safe…not yet.

Theodora's momentary surprise didn't last long. She hurled a blazing magical cannonball at them as the bike flew off.

"Look out!" Charlee yelled.

The bike veered to the left just as Theodora's magic shot by. The fiery round grazed Charlee's thigh, burning through her pants, down to skin. "Owww!" Smoke rose from the charred skin, the stench, like rotten eggs. Charlee shivered, her head became wobbly, eyes closed. *No! Don't pass out. You can't.*

More of Theodora's attack shook the bike, awakening Charlee. "Bike, get us out of here!" she commanded.

The bike dove sharply toward the street below. Charlee held onto Sandra as the cool night air whipped by, rousing her further from the wooziness caused by the burn. The bike maintained its high-speed dive. The street rushed at them. Charlee screamed. So did Sandra. They were going to crash. At that speed, how could the bike pull up in time? But it did, leveling off and gliding between the buildings. It darted from one skyscraper to the next, getting as far from Theodora as possible. As the sorceress disappeared from view, Charlee eased back in the seat—until her great-aunt's voice filled her mind.

You fool! You think you have escaped me? You haven't. I have simply allowed you to flee. The sickening words echoed in Charlee's mind. *We are blood. I can see your every move. Nothing has changed. I still want my medallion, and you are going to bring it to me. If you have not returned it to me by the time the Queen of the Night rises again to full glory, these insignificant creatures you care so much about…these and many more…will become my slaves forever. They will be beasts with no purpose other than to serve me. Maybe I will start with your little friend. What is her name? Sandra!*

"No!"

"Charlee, you okay?" Sandra's voice came as if in a dream. "Charlee, answer me!"

"Yeah…I'm fine," she finally answered, but she wasn't. Her dad was badly hurt and her home destroyed. Theodora had already threatened her family and now Sandra, her best friend, was in danger. She couldn't let Sandra take any more risks. "Bike, take us back to Sandra's house."

"What?" Sandra cried in sharp protest.

Charlee didn't respond.

Chapter 17

Feeling Lost

The bike landed in a park not far from Sandra's house. Charlee barely climbed off before her friend threw her arms around her. They hugged for several moments before Sandra broke from the embrace. "You shouldn't have gone after Theodora by yourself, Charlee. She could have killed you. Look at your leg."

Charlee glanced at the wound. Actually, thanks to the bike's energy, the charred skin had already started to heal. "Sandra, what did you do?"

"I saved your butt. What else?"

"Yes, but how'd you get out? I thought your dad—"

"I know what you said to him. Thanks a lot. You almost got me grounded. Luckily, my dad can never stay mad at me. Plus, I know a lot of tricks to get out of the house. He may know how to catch criminals, but he doesn't know how to stop me when I'm determined to do something."

"Yeah, but how'd you—"

"Get the bike to fly? I didn't do anything. After I snuck out of the house, I used my cell to call a taxi. My dad would kill me if he knew that, but he's going to kill me anyway, so what the heck. When I reached…you know… your building, that freak thunderstorm was going on."

"You could see that? It wasn't just me?" Charlee interrupted. Overhead the storm clouds had parted. The sky was clear again as the moon brightened the night.

"I guess the whole city could see it," Sandra answered. "It blew in so suddenly. That's a strange question."

"It's just that earlier there was a fog around the building that no one seemed to see. So why could everyone see the storm?" Charlee looked back at the city's skyscrapers and scratched her head.

"Maybe it's because the witch was really pissed and wanted to freak out everyone," Sandra reasoned. "Let me continue my story."

Charlee nodded.

Sandra gripped the bike's handlebar. "When I got to the building and looked up, the next thing I knew, your bike swooped from the sky with those crazy wings and picked me up. It must have been going to your rescue when it spotted me. Your bike's smarter than you. It knew I could help you. All I did was grab the handlebars and hold on."

Charlee glared at the bike. It had retracted its wings so once again it disguised itself as an aging heap of junk.

"That's some bike, Charlee."

"Sandra, you shouldn't have come."

"That's the thanks I get for saving you from that witch!" Sandra released the bike and stepped closer to Charlee.

"Sandra, stop! You didn't save me. All you've done is make things worse. That witch is going to hurt a lot of people unless I can find a way to stop her." Charlee, her leg sore, leaned against a tree. "And now she knows who you are. She knows you're my friend. That means she's going to come looking for you. You're in danger."

"Charlee—"

"No, listen. How am I supposed to keep you safe and stop Theodora at the same time?"

"Don't worry about protecting me." Sandra's eyes flared, jaw tightened. "I don't need your protection. I don't need anyone. If Theodora comes knocking, it'll be her mistake."

"This isn't a joke, Sandra."

"Charlee, I know."

"Look, go home. You can't help me anymore." Charlee avoided Sandra's stare, gazing at the grass.

"Charlee, listen—"

"Just go before you make things worse." Charlee pushed away from the tree and folded her arms.

Shaking her head, Sandra backed away slowly and then turned to run. She stopped only once next to the bike, removed something from around her neck, and placed it on the bike's handlebars. Then she was gone.

Charlee slumped onto the grass, trembling in the crisp San Francisco night. She had hurt Sandra, but it had to be done. She couldn't risk her friend's life. Sandra would understand. "No she won't. She's a fighter. She's handling this so much better than me."

Lifting herself from the grass, she limped to the ugly two-wheeler. "What have you done, bike?" She stood over it, poised to kick and knock it over—anything to punish the bike for involving Sandra—but she stopped. A thin gold chain with a small golden cross pendant hung on the handlebars. Sandra's gold necklace. It was the one that belonged to her grandmother. *Why'd she leave it? So her grandmother would watch over me? Protect me?* Charlee removed the pendant from the handlebars and slid it into the one remaining pant pocket that survived Theodora's magical assault, ready to guard the pendant with her life.

Charlee refocused her frustration on the bike. "Where do you get off having wings? Why didn't you tell me you could fly? Why don't you tell me anything? What am I supposed to do now? Come on, stupid bike! Tell me something. Tell me!"

The bike remained silent.

"Dumb bike, I thought we were a team. You know what? I wish you'd just go away!" She tried to push the bike over but couldn't budge it. After several attempts, she sat in the grass and tears came.

"Bike, I'm sorry. I just don't know what to do." For a second, she thought about seeking help from her mom who always had answers. She reached for her cell phone, which…she suddenly realized…had been inside the burned pant pocket. Gone. "What do I do now?"

Though not expecting it, she received an answer. "Don't give up."

§ § §

"Tribon!" Charlee stood just as the red-bearded giant emerged from the darkness. He held his massive sword so that its long blade rested casually on his shoulder. "Tribon, am I glad to see you. I've made a mess of everything. I don't know what to do. I'm not cut out for this—I'm just a girl, not some knight. You fight Theodora!"

"If only I could. But I have no way of reaching your world. Remember, I'm only with you in spirit, brought here by the power of your mind." Tribon took a long stride closer to Charlee.

"Well, let me try to open a gateway." Her voice quivered.

"I'm sorry, young knight. You still lack the power. You require more time to recover your strength, especially as I see you already have been injured in battle." He pointed to her burned leg.

"I feel strong though." Charlee tried to cover the charred mark with a hand.

"That may be. But if you attempt to open the gateway prematurely, you could cause damage. I can't allow you to take the risk. You are the one destined to face Theodora. You must be physically and mentally strong for the challenge."

"You don't understand. I faced Theodora. She demanded that I find the medallion and give it to her by tomorrow night when the full moon rises again or else she'll hurt people. I don't know where to begin to look. I wouldn't even know the medallion if I saw it. I don't know what it looks like."

"Nor do I." Tribon took a few steps as if pacing. "I have only heard of its power but never set eyes on it. Search your mind, young knight. I know you will find the answer. You are of the bloodline of the greatest guardian. Trust in the blood coursing through your veins. It will lead you to the medallion." He stopped to stroke his long beard. "You must find the medallion for it is the only weapon that can help you stop Theodora."

"You said that before, when we met at the school. You said I could use its power. But how?"

"Young knight, you must discover that for yourself. Have faith. All is not yet lost. But you must move quickly. Even without the medallion, Theodora will begin her conquest by hurting those closest to you. She will turn people into her slaves—her monsters. She will devastate Earth just as she has Janasara. The woman has no soul. She sold it to become a master of the dark arts."

"Thanks for the pep talk," Charlee said coolly.

"I do not understand."

"Never mind. Tribon, you didn't tell me Theodora was my great-aunt. You didn't tell me my mom is the daughter of the Guardian Michala. Why not? I don't get any of this. I don't even know who I am anymore."

"You are right." Tribon bowed his head and gritted his teeth. "I should have been more open with you. I thought if you knew too much, it might weaken your resolve. Now that you know, you must put aside your fear and confusion and focus on the task ahead. There will be time to understand more soon, should you survive."

Charlee placed a hand in her one good pocket and touched Sandra's gold cross. "Listen, I'll try to find the medallion. When I do, be ready to make the jump across the gateway. You have to help me."

"We shall see. But remember, it is your destiny as the Last Guardian that calls to you now."

"I hate when you say that. I never asked for this."

"It is a burden placed upon you by fate. Don't fail the people of this world. Find the medallion. Use its power."

With these words, Tribon strolled into the darkened park.

"Hey! Don't leave!"

"I will always be with you."

The giant knight soon faded. Charlee felt alone, but at the same time a flicker of determination was kindled. She had a mission: find the medallion and use it against Theodora.

Charlee climbed onto the bike. "I'm sorry for everything, bike. I'm sorry for not thanking you for saving my life…again. Thanks for staying by my side."

In response, the bike's white wings sprung from the frame and rose above her head. Charlee grinned slightly. "Bike, let's fly."

Chapter 18

One More Battle

Flashes of red lit the night over the city's skyscrapers. Sirens raced toward the bursts. Theodora was at it again. The medallion would have to wait.

"Bike, whatever she's doing…we have to stop her." Together, Charlee and her winged companion flew back to the financial district.

They landed on the roof of a skyscraper at the edge of the district. Theodora hovered over the city a few blocks away. Red beams coursed from bony fingers, randomly striking people still roaming downtown despite the late hour. A woman struck by a bolt dropped to her knees, shook, twisted, cried out, and then mutated into a beast. In her place was a creature with yellow eyes, a long snout, and fangs…like a werewolf. The beast howled as if in pain. It whirled in each direction then bounded up the street, running on its hind legs.

Charlee lowered her head against the handlebars. "Theodora said she would enslave the people of Earth," she mumbled. "Bike, take us closer but be careful to stay out of Theodora's sight."

The bike jetted into the air, using the surrounding buildings as cover. Charlee scanned the street. She counted maybe ten of the strange, werewolf-like creatures lumbering around, but the numbers were increasing. A bolt hit what may have been a homeless man pushing a shopping cart loaded with trash bags. He dropped to the ground as the change overcame him. His yellow eyes seemed lost as if he waited for a command—Theodora's command. All the monsters shared that lost expression in their wolf faces.

"How do I stop this?" Charlee leaned on the bike, closed her eyes, and slowed her breathing. A thought flashed through her mind, like a mushrooming firework explosion on the Fourth of July. *Ram her! Strike her down—now!*

"Bike, go!" The bike climbed to a higher altitude. Its breakneck speed would have caused another rider to lose their grip and fall helplessly to the street, but Charlee was in synch with the bike. They moved as one, thought as one.

The bike soared as if charging toward the moon, then swung in a wide arch and looped back down toward Theodora for the collision.

"She'll never see us coming. We might not survive—but neither will she. We can end this right now!" Charlee cried. The bike increased its speed as they rushed toward Theodora. No way was the sorceress going to see them coming.

"We're going do it!" Charlee tensed each muscle. They were close now... very close. In another second they would end Theodora's attack on the city.

Come on! Here we go! Charlee stood on the pedals and leaned forward. She counted down the seconds. *Three...two...one!* Then Theodora, her eyes still focused on the street below, raised a hand toward them.

Their charge came to a sudden, jarring halt as if an invisible net snared them. The shock threw Charlee from the bike. Dazed, she and the bike hurtled toward the concrete below. Her mind focused seconds away from a splattered, messy ending. "No!" she screamed as her arms and legs thrashed wildly, but death never came. The sorceress magically snatched them up just inches above the street, lassoing them with an invisible rope.

Charlee breathed deeply, clearing her head. A chill rose up her back, body shivered. Theodora was just so strong. "How can I stop her?" Charlee winced as the sorceress—just a few feet away now—tightened the invisible rope, crushing her arms. A wide smile crossed Theodora's aged face, revealing jagged yellow teeth.

"What?" Charlee asked.

"A valiant effort, young fool! Have you not learned that you cannot defeat me? You have but one choice. Bring me the medallion, or these simple creatures will all become my slaves."

"Look, you don't need to do this." Charlee wrestled against Theodora's clutch. "I'll find the medallion. I promise. Give me a chance."

"Oh, I know you will do as I say. You have no choice. But I thought a little reminder was called for after you and that girl so rudely left our earlier discussion. I ask you, was that right? I think not. I think you should not test me."

To emphasize the point, lightning shot from Theodora's hands, strafing windows of a nearby skyscraper. Glass and debris rained down on the street, shattering against the concrete with an ear-piercing crack that never seemed to end. Screams of those not yet transformed rippled across several blocks. Cars came to a screeching halt. The city was under attack and the explosive chorus of horrors rang in Charlee's ears. Police sirens blared as officers aimed their weapons skyward at both her and Theodora and at the wolf creatures running along the street. Any moment police might open fire and kill those poor people.

"Stop!" Charlee demanded.

"I will not. Not until what is rightfully mine is back in my hands." Theodora hesitated. Her head drooped...just for a moment. Was she weakening? Was she gathering her strength? The moment didn't last. "Remember, you must bring me the medallion when the Queen of the Night rises to the peak of her kingdom once again. Should you fail, these souls who have volunteered to join my grand army will be forever altered. And they are just the beginning."

Charlee glared at Theodora. "When I bring the medallion, you'll return these people to normal and leave?"

"You dare question me? You are in no position to ask such questions. Now go. You have much to accomplish. The lives of everyone in this kingdom are in your hands. Fail me, and the first to suffer will be that insolent girl. She will be followed by your mother—my dear, sweet niece—and then your sister and your father."

"Fine…whatever." Charlee's heart fluttered. Visions of her injured dad returned, then her mom and Megan. She had endangered them all. "Just tell me how I find you when I have the medallion?"

"Do not worry about such trivialities. You will know how to find me when the time is right."

"Then let me go, so I can find your stupid medallion."

Theodora nodded. "As you wish." The sorceress drew back her hand and slung Charlee and the bike clear across the city. They hurtled uncontrollably through the night. But this time, Theodora was not going to stop their fall. The bike spun out of control, its wings flailing uselessly. It seemed…unconscious. *Have to…wake it…up…or we…die!* Charlee reached out for the bike. She had to snag a handlebar, a pedal, a wing—anything to make contact.

Come on! Reach. Reach! Reach! The city rushed by beneath her. She flew by one rooftop, then another. She craned her neck to glance ahead. *Oh my God!* A skyscraper stood directly in their path. They would smash into the glass exterior in seconds. *Try…again! Reach for the bike! Reach!*

The fingers of her right hand touched the handlebars. Then she got a full grip and pulled herself onto the banana seat, but the bike did not respond to her presence. "Bike, wake up!" No response. "Bike, we're going to die!" Nothing. She steadied herself. This time, instead of shouting, she used thought to communicate. She willed it to regain consciousness. *Bike, please! Wake up!*

The building neared, the offices inside—tables, chairs, computers, cleaning crews—all visible. Charlee tugged at the handlebars. *Now bike!* The bike rocked itself back to life, extending its wings to their fullest length. The movement propelled it into a one-hundred-and-eighty-degree turn just as its tires bounced off the glass panels on the side of a building, shattering them. In the next heartbeat, it pulled itself away and came to a stop, hovering in mid-air.

Charlee slumped over the frame, utterly exhausted. She wanted to give into the desire to sleep as unconsciousness beckoned her. It would be so easy to close her eyes. "Come on, wake up, Charlee. This isn't finished," she told herself.

"Bike, we have to try again." She sat up in the seat, griping the handlebars tight. "We have to stop her from turning any more people into those wolf-things. If we don't, police are going to start shooting and people will be hurt…or worse."

With an explosive thrust of its wings, the bike shot back to the spot where they had challenged Theodora. The situation had worsened. Police barricaded a whole city block. Officers clad in battle gear with helmets, shields and batons lined the street with their handguns and assault rifles aimed at the once-human, now wolf-like creatures. The monsters no longer wandered aimless and confused through the streets. Like the police, they had lined up in formation—an army waiting for an order to attack.

"Dive down there, bike," Charlee commanded. "We have to make the police understand what's happening. Swoop down, but do it slowly. We don't want them shooting at us." The bike folded its wings straight back and leaned into a controlled dive toward the scene below.

"Don't shoot! They're human!" Charlee waved her arms while shouting. Catching sight of the winged bike rushing at them, the police aimed their weapons at the bike—and her.

"Bike, stop just in front of the officers," Charlee whispered, raising her hands to show she was unarmed. They landed softly then rolled to a stop just a few feet in front of squad cars. Sliding from the frame, hands still in the air, she took careful steps toward the police. Clicks sounded in unison—the music of rifles armed and ready. Long barrels had her targeted, as though a bull's-eye marked her chest.

"Don't shoot! Please! Don't hurt these creatures. They're people. This isn't their fault. It's mine." Charlee inched toward the officers.

"Down on your stomach," one officer ordered. "Hands behind your—"

"Sergeant, I will handle this." From the crowd of police Mr. Flores, Sandra's dad, emerged. The deputy chief, bullhorn in one hand, handgun in the other, stared at her with angry, disbelieving eyes. Without saying a word he holstered his gun, grabbed Charlee by the arm, and dragged her to a gathering of squad cars. "I knew there was something I wasn't going to like about you."

"Mr. Flores, you have to listen."

"Listen to what?" he asked, releasing her arm. "One moment, I'm at home with my family, and the next moment I get a call about werewolves, or some kind of beasts straight out of a nightmare, loose in the city."

He snatched a pair of binoculars from one officer and spied the creatures. They remained in formation but were growing increasingly aggressive. They howled into the night, bared their long fangs, and arched their backs.

"Then," Mr. Flores continued, "out of nowhere some kid on a flying bike shows up. And that kid turns out to be my daughter's new friend. What can you tell me about this insanity? And where did you get a flying bike?"

Charlee swallowed a mouthful of saliva. "I don't have time to explain everything right now. But listen, those aren't beasts. They're people. You can't shoot them. They've been turned into those monsters by a...a sorceress...and it's because of me. I let it happen. Now I have to stop her and you've got to find a way to keep those people safe until I can end this."

"This is nuts." Mr. Flores again grabbed her by the arm. "That's it, I'm hauling you off to juvenile hall, and I'm going to take these...these things... out any way I can."

"Mr. Flores, please!" Charlee pleaded.

"Listen to her, Dad."

Charlee swung around when she heard Sandra's voice. Her friend stood between two officers, as if she was someone of royalty to the police.

"Sandra!" Charlee shook free of Mr. Flores and bounded over to her friend.

"What...how...how did you get out here?" Mr. Flores' eyes bulged.

"Sir, somehow she snuck past those beasts," one of the officers standing beside Sandra explained. "I recognized her as your—"

"Dad, you have to do whatever Charlee says," Sandra blurted before the officer finished. "Everything she is telling you is true. Believe me."

"Sands." Mr. Flores rubbed his chin gruffly.

"Dad." Sandra held his stare.

Mr. Flores softened. "Lieutenant," the deputy chief called to one of his commanders, "spread the word. The creatures are not to be harmed. Use non-lethal force, nothing else. And find a way to round them up—fast—before word gets out."

"Uh, how, sir?" the lieutenant asked.

"Get me headquarters. We need a helicopter and as many tranquilizer guns as we can find."

"Sir? Tranquilizer guns?"

"Just do it! Hit the city zoo. We need the stuff that could knock out a bear...better yet, an elephant."

"Yes, sir."

"And Lieutenant, we need to do this now and do it quietly. We need these people...these creatures...off the streets."

As the lieutenant nodded, Mr. Flores placed his bullhorn to his mouth and ordered all his officers to lower their weapons until given further orders. He then returned his attention to his daughter and Charlee.

"I don't know what's going on here, but I guess I have no choice but to believe you. When this is over though, you're going to have a great deal of explaining to do. And I might still throw your butt in juvie for bringing this chaos to my city."

"Yes, sir." Charlee lowered her eyes.

"Now, what can the Police Department do to help bust this sorceress? You can't do this alone."

"She's not alone." Sandra stepped forward. "I'll be with her."

Charlee was going to call out 'no,' but Mr. Flores spoke first. "No way, Sands! You are going home where you should have been in the first place."

He motioned to the two officers standing beside Sandra. "Please escort my daughter home. Don't leave my residence until you see my wife has charge of her."

Charlee clasped Sandra's hand. "Thanks for being there...again." Sandra smiled but said nothing as the officers led her away. Charlee then stared at Mr. Flores. "I have to do this alone."

On cue, the bike flew over, came to a landing on the roof of a nearby patrol unit and lowered a wing. She grabbed the feathers and climbed onto the bike's seat. "Just keep these people safe," she urged as the bike rose into the sky.

Mr. Flores shook his head. "Maybe we should call in the military."

"If I blow it anymore, you might have to." Charlee peered toward the horizon as the bike took flight. The moon would soon slip away, giving rise to a new dawn.

The truth was not even the military could stop Theodora.

"Theodora! Face me again!" Charlee called out as the bike zoomed over the high rises. She waited for a response. None came. "Come on, witch! This is between you and me—no one else. Remember, it was my bloodline that stole your immortality. Come and get me."

The sorceress still did not respond—had no reason to. Why waste time in another battle? The order was clear...find the medallion. There was no choice. Charlee had to find it and she had to do it fast. Perhaps the new day would bring hope. If she failed, it might bring the world's darkest hour.

Chapter 19

Answers Deep Inside

Thirteen hours till nightfall. That was how much time she had to find the medallion—the only weapon that could destroy Theodora.

Charlee and the bike soared across a pale morning sky just now touched by the sun's first rays. The bike flew in no particular direction, giving her time to think. How could she find the medallion when she had no idea where to begin?

She breathed in the sweet morning air, blinking away the sleep that still beckoned. Off toward the Bay, a morning fog snaked its way inland, like the doubt that crept into her thoughts.

Charlee frowned. "Even if by some miracle I find this silly medallion, how can I learn to use it against Theodora? Maybe I shouldn't try. Maybe I should just give her the dumb thing and hope she goes back to her own world. What did Tribon call it? Janasara?"

No. There was no choice. She had to find the medallion and use it. But where should she start looking? "Tribon, where are you when I need you?"

A silent breeze provided no answer. Oh well, at least she had the bike. Its power surged through her, giving strength—but what good had it done? She hadn't stopped Theodora. And how many new abilities did she really gain from the bike? Charlee had no idea what she was capable of...no idea what the bike was capable of, and she had no time to figure it out. She had to remain focused on the medallion.

Her head spinning from so many questions, she laid down on the handlebars. Then a soft voice rose from somewhere deep within her mind. *Relax. Just breathe. Do not think. Let go, and all that you seek to know will be revealed.*

"Who is that?" Charlee asked. "Is that you, bike? Are you talking to me through my mind?" Silence followed. Call it a gut instinct, but she didn't think the bike had spoken, and it didn't seem like her own subconscious speaking. Charlee took a long breath. "Maybe I should listen. I've nothing to lose."

She concentrated on rhythmic breaths, counting each time she captured and released a lungful of air. *One, two, three, in. One, two, three, out.* Her muscles relaxed, thoughts silenced. She heard nothing as if sealed in a cocoon. The emptiness brought peace until…a sudden picture exploded like someone had snapped a photograph with a massive flash bulb inches away. It forced her eyes open. Charlee jerked up. "What was that?" She didn't need an answer. She knew exactly what the image was. The medallion!

Shutting her eyes once again, she focused harder on the vision. A medallion the size of a mini-Frisbee, just a bit larger than her hand, spun slowly. It was made of a pitch black stone that swallowed light. One side was engraved with the image of a burning tree. As the medallion rotated, it revealed another engraving on the other.

Charlee couldn't quite make it out at first. She plunged farther into her mind, thoughts like fingertips almost touching the medallion. She had to see it but at the same time, a knot in her stomach warned of danger. The engraving became clear. It was a face. Her face! A twisted version of herself years from now! Scarred, angry and evil! *What?* Why would her face be on the medallion?

A jolt from the bike brought Charlee back to reality. What did it mean? Was she going to become evil? And how did the image get in her head? She had never seen the medallion before. She had no memory of her dad or mom ever speaking of it, although she wished they had. Though the morning was bright, the inescapable gloom of the vision surrounded her just as the fog surrounded the Bay.

"Bike, I saw it…the medallion! I know what it looks like!" She didn't mention the vision of her warped face. Why speak of it? It might not be her face at all. "But I still don't know where to find it." She fought the urge to scream.

Scanning the slowly awakening city below, Charlee thought of the poor people who had been mutated into Theodora's slaves. She hoped Mr. Flores and the Police Department had been able to round them up without harming anyone. Soon the entire city would be awake, everyone unaware of the danger they faced…because of her. What about her family? Had Theodora already reached her mom and sister, like her dad?

"I should go find them—see if they're all right," she said as if speaking to the bike. "I should talk to Mom. Find out why she never told me. If she had, maybe none of this would have happened. Maybe Dad—"

Charlee tightened her grip on the handlebars. "Wait a second! Dad was attacked in his office at the university. Theodora thought he had the medallion, but he wouldn't give it to her and she didn't find it. That's why she beat him. It could still be there!" Right now she had no other ideas.

Chapter 20

The Clue

Charlee surveyed the remains of her dad's office as she wiped away the dust and cobwebs from the air duct she had crawled through. Since it was a weekend and the building was locked, she decided to enter the room through the air duct rather than break into the building through a doorway or locked window. She didn't want to risk setting off an alarm. The bike had flown her to the roof where she made quick work of tearing open an air duct to enter the building.

Finding the office proved challenging. After dropping into the air duct, she crawled for what seemed an eternity. After a half dozen wrong turns, she peered through an office vent and spotted a familiar scarf on the floor. It was white with pink stripes with her dad's initials stitched in blue letters. It was the one she knitted for him during summer camp years ago. She knew then she had found the right one.

The signs of struggle provided more proof. A bookshelf lay on the ground crushed into pieces. Books littered the floor. Burn marks scarred the walls.

If there was anything important to find here—like a medallion—she hoped the police hadn't already found it. Then again, if Theodora was unsuccessful, police likely hadn't either.

One question danced in her mind. "Why does she need me to find this medallion, anyway?" Tribon called it her immortality. Shouldn't she have a special connection to it? Shouldn't she be able to sniff it out, like a dog? Charlee pondered this until an answer formed. "Maybe, just maybe, her powers are weaker on Earth. Maybe she can't sense the medallion here. If that's true, maybe I can beat her."

Sitting in the chair at her dad's desk, she imagined Theodora flinging him across the office, slamming him into the bookcase. Gouges marked the wooden desk and charred black spots covered the walls. Theodora's energy blasts.

"How was Dad able to keep the medallion hidden? Maybe he doesn't really know where it is. No, he must know and risked his life to keep it hidden. But why did Theodora let him live? Maybe, she didn't think he would survive." Charlee slammed her hands on the desk. "I'm sorry, Dad."

Her mind continued to spill over details. What was it Theodora had said? *As my great-niece, you could have joined me. You could have learned from me. You could have had everything your heart desires.* Maybe, Theodora never intended to hurt her in their first confrontation atop the skyscraper.

"She wants me at her side to teach me all her creepy sorcery. Maybe that's why she didn't kill Dad. She knows if she were to kill anyone in my family, I would never join her. But why choose me?" The answer to that question would have to wait.

The vision returned of her twisted and aged face on the medallion. Was she doomed to become evil? If the medallion comes from the dark arts, like Tribon said, would using it change her? Regardless of her fate, she had no choice but to find the medallion and destroy Theodora with it. Time was running out.

"All right, where would you hide it, Dad?" She searched the office. "There must be a secret compartment here somewhere. Think like Dad."

She pulled open the desk drawers but found only the papers he had been grading. She checked under the desk. Nothing. Could it be under the floor? If only she had x-ray vision.

"Maybe I do." Her super eyesight—perhaps it would work like x-ray vision if she focused.

Concentrating, she looked around the office one more time, trying to peer through the floor and walls but she couldn't penetrate the solids. Still, sharp details revealed themselves, like an ever-so-slight variation in the color of a section of the right wall.

The color variation, though subtle, was perceptible just beyond the outline of a poster for an upcoming Renaissance faire. Two different shades of beige had been used, as if someone had repainted the wall and almost gotten the color perfect.

Heart thumping fast, she walked to the wall and ripped off the poster. The lighter-colored section covered an area slightly larger than the poster. She felt around the edge of the area, but found no notch or mark that would indicate a way to remove the wall panel.

"Nothing left to do but punch a hole through the wall." Charlee clenched a fist, still sensing the bike's power, and crashed through it as though it were made of paper. Ripping away plaster and wood, her eyes widened as she found a shelf had been placed between the beams. It held a plain wooden box, which Charlee carefully removed. Cradling it with one hand, she used the other to lift the lid, and she peeked inside. A book…only a book. Hopes for finding the medallion shattered.

"A book!" she muttered, shaking her head in disgust. "Leave it to Dad to hide a book in the wall."

She stared at the book's cracked, bent cover. After a few sulky moments, reason returned. "Why would Dad hide a book in a wall?" She sat at the desk and thumbed through the pages. Her dad's writing filled page after page. Each entry was inscribed with a date.

"It's a journal." This could be a treasure. "Hmmm, why did Dad feel the need to stash this journal behind a wall?" The last entry was dated about a month after he had moved the family to San Francisco. She read the entry.

"I know this move has been hard on my daughter, and I can only hope that someday she will forgive me for taking her away from the home she's known all her life. As she nears adulthood and comes to know who she really is…should she possess the power her mother and I believe dwells inside her…I must do all I can to protect her. I must hide her. I felt I could do that better in the city where there are hundreds of thousands of people. We can become lost among the masses, just another family in suburbia. I hope this works. Still, I fear for Charlee and for my family. I wish I could share with her all that I know, but there are things she must learn for herself, free from any intervention. Otherwise, she might never realize her full abilities."

Charlee closed the book. They had moved because of her. "Dad was trying to protect me, probably from Theodora. But what's all this about powers and abilities? Was he talking about the whole guardian thing? Or is there more?" Her vision blurred. "I've been such a jerk. I didn't know. I didn't understand."

She took a breath and searched the book again, hoping to find a clue to the medallion's whereabouts. Poetry and her dad's musings on life filled the pages. Nothing about a medallion!

Her dad tried, more than once, to teach her about poetry where words were laced with all kinds of unexpected meanings. They could symbolize more than they seemed to say. If that was the case here, she would have to study the journal for days, weeks, months to find any clue of the medallion—if any existed. She didn't have the time. Hours remained and even they quickly slipped away.

Come on! Charlee nearly flung the journal across the office. She stopped herself just as a piece of paper fell from the pages to the floor. It was a stub of an admission ticket that had already been used. The ticket was to the city's Museum of World History, and it was dated not long after they moved to the city.

101

Could this stub be meaningful? Why else would her dad take such care to place it in a journal and stash the journal in a hole hidden in the wall? Why else would he seal the hole up so that he could never again read his own writings?

Or, perhaps it had marked a particular page of sappy poetry. Then again, maybe it had marked an important page with a key clue. Now she would never know. No! That ticket stub itself must be the clue! At this point, it was all she had. "I'm going to the museum," she decided.

Now, how to get out of the building? She glanced up at the open air duct, but it wasn't an option. She didn't want to go back in there with the spiders and cobwebs.

She stepped toward the office door. Voices sounded just outside the door. She listened closely. "I want the room dusted again," one voice said. "There has to be some clue in there as to who attacked Dr. Smelton. I'm not going to allow any further attacks like this at my university. Is that clear?"

"Yes, chief," another voice said. "But don't you think we should wait for the go-ahead from the police?"

"This campus is our jurisdiction," the first voice responded. "I don't want the city to think the campus police can't handle this investigation. Now find me some answers—and I mean today."

Charlee had to move quickly. She spun around to face the only possible escape route—the window. She pulled open the blinds. The bike hovered outside the window, its spread wings flapping just enough to keep it in place.

"Bike, great timing!" Charlee whispered. She unlocked the window, swung it open, and then climbed onto the banana seat. "We've got to get to the Museum of World History. Fast!"

§ § §

Riding rather than flying to avoid attention, Charlee took a detour before heading to the museum. "Bike, let's stop at the hospital and check on Dad." She prayed he was better. She could also talk with Mom…really talk about all that had happened and about why so many secrets in the family.

When they arrived at the hospital, Charlee started to run for the entrance. She stopped though and returned to the bike. "Please don't disappear." She placed a hand on the frame. "Keep your eyes…well, eye…open for anything. Theodora could be anywhere."

Charlee dashed inside the hospital back up to the intensive care unit to the room where she had last found her dad. Pushing the door to Room 304, she stood paralyzed. Empty! Mom…Dad…Megan, all gone! Had Theodora got to them? *No, please, no!* Charlee bolted from the room to the nursing station. "My dad…where is he!"

A nurse peered over the computer. "Sorry, dear, who are you asking about?"

"My, dad…uh, Joseph Smelton…he was in Room 304, but he's gone." Charlee tapped on the counter with all her fingers. She whirled in every direction, searching the ICU as she waited for the nurse to answer.

"Let me see, honey." The nurse clicked on the computer terminal then she grimaced. "I'm sorry. Who did you say you were?"

"I'm his daughter, Charlee Smelton! Please, you have to tell me what happened! Why's he not here?"

The nurse stared sternly at Charlee. "According to the last nursing report, your father checked out of the hospital several hours ago on his own consent, but he did so against the doctor's recommendation. Dear, your father had serious injuries and he is endangering himself by not being in the hospital."

Charlee shook her head. It didn't make any sense. He was too injured to leave the hospital on his own. Was this Theodora's doing? Had she gotten to them all? *Home! I have to get home!*

Hurrying from the hospital, Charlee reached the bike. "Get me home. There's no time to waste. We have to fly." The bike spread its wings, stretching its feathers out to the late morning sun. They quickly shot into the sky. People below pointed at the girl on the flying bike. She didn't care anymore. She had to find her family…had to make sure they were safe.

The bike rocketed to the house, but it still felt like an eternity. What would she find? More messages from Theodora vowing to kill her family? Or would she find worse? Charlee didn't want to think about it.

As they descended toward the house, yellow police tape over the doorway became visible. When the bike landed, Charlee ducked under the tape and ran through the burned entrance. "Mom? Dad? Megan? Anyone here? Are you guys all right? Someone please answer me." She ran through the house stumbling over debris. No one answered. No one greeted her.

Charlee sprinted up the stairs first to her empty parents' room and then to her own. She stopped at her dresser and stared at a broken picture of her family. They weren't here, but where could they be?

"I've had enough of this." Raising her tightly clenched fists above her head, she brought them crashing down on the dresser. The thick would split in half. "Theodora, get ready. I'm coming for you."

Chapter 21

The Middle Ages Await

After a clothes change and fixing her wind-swept hair into a pony tail, she headed on the bike toward the museum. They zipped along the city streets, dodging cars and people, creating a whoosh of wind that swept trash and dust airborne in their wake.

On the way, a calming voice filled her thoughts. *Your family is safe. Do not fear for them. They are always with you.*

"Is that you, Tribon?"

She received no response although it didn't sound like the giant knight. She couldn't even tell if the words, spoken in little more than a whisper, came from a male or female. Maybe it was her subconscious...maybe something more.

She leaned in closer to the handlebars. "Bike, better slow down. We're close. Let's stop a block from the museum and scope it out." They slowed among some of the smaller banks and businesses on the outskirts of San Francisco's financial district, only a few blocks from the high rises where she battled with Theodora last night.

The museum rose ahead. Charlee pedaled along a sidewalk, her brow furrowed. The streets buzzed with Saturday morning activity, but after the night's terror this part of the city should be empty. Shouldn't people be in hiding after all that transpired during the dark hours? What about the police barricade? What about all the people who were turned into Theodora's slaves? They were questions Charlee could not answer.

She climbed from the bike and pushed it to a nearby newsstand. While the clerk chatted with a taxi driver, she grabbed one of the day's newspapers and glanced through it. The paper had nothing about last night's battle. *Of course!* Charlee reasoned mentally. *It happened too late to get into the newspapers. But the TV news, the radio—they must have something.*

Close by, the newsstand clerk had a portable television tuned to the news. Charlee listened carefully. The anchorwoman spoke of an early-morning police incident.

"City police armed with riot gear barricaded a financial district street early today, responding to calls about a wild costume party that turned violent. Party-goers damaged cars and broke windows. There were reports of several arrests before police gained control of the situation. More information is expected to become available later today."

Charlee smiled. Clever, Mr. Flores! He'd managed to cover up what really occurred. Chances are the police wouldn't be able to keep it hidden for much longer. The press was going to get wind of the story.

"But what about the Internet?" Charlee wondered out loud. Someone must have shot video on a cell phone. How long before it was all over the web? Maybe it already was. And the police were probably inundated with missing-person calls about the people changed by Theodora who never returned home.

Hopefully, they wouldn't have to worry about it for long. Hopefully, the city would be safe before the next sunrise. She couldn't fail.

"Hey, kid! You have to pay for that." She flinched at the clerk's harsh voice and dropped the newspaper.

"Sorry." She wheeled the bike across the street to the museum and stopped at the steps leading up to the entrance. "This has to be it. This has to be where the medallion is."

The grand stone steps ended in front of a marble entryway with a massive, dark-glass doorway. Above the entrance flew flags from every country, a sign of the museum's international theme. The six-story building took up nearly a whole city block.

"Bike, stay here," Charlee whispered, trying not to attract attention. "But be ready to move at any moment."

The little hairs on the back of her neck stood; someone watched her. She turned around but spotted nothing—at least no one of suspicion...just a city street full of people minding their own business.

"I don't know where Theodora is right now, but she's got to be close." She knelt down so that her eyes were even with the reflector. "I know she's close. I wish I could take you in there with me, but I can't. I need you to be my eyes out here." Charlee held onto the bike a bit longer. It was her lifeline. Releasing her companion was tough, but she had to climb the stone steps to the museum alone.

At the great glass doorway, she hesitated before pulling it open. "Dad, I hope I understood your clue," she uttered. "Please let the medallion be here. If it's not I'm screwed. I don't know where else to look."

As the doors opened, Charlee gasped at the huge museum complex. It was like a city within a city. The lobby was lined with models of the Seven Wonders of the World from the Coliseum in Rome to the Pyramids of Egypt and the Great Wall of China—all towering over her head. At the far end was a rotating model of the Earth, sitting atop a marble stone base. Murals of people from around the world covered the walls. The ceiling was cut out from the lobby's center and the levels above, revealing an expansive view of all six stories. A glass elevator and a spiraling staircase both climbed the museum while escalators provided another access to each floor. A chorus of voices resonated throughout the museum as crowds ascended from the lobby to the higher floors.

Charlee had been to the museum before, but she didn't remember it being this big. But last time she wasn't on a hunt for a magical weapon that could save the world—or destroy it.

If the medallion was here, it would take her a year to find it—unless, of course, she could focus to figure it out. Now more than ever, she wished Sandra was at her side. Gazing one more time at all six stories as she walked farther into the museum's lobby, Charlee started to feel small and insignificant.

"Young lady, do you have a ticket?" A burly security guard stepped into her path. The man was so big that he resembled Tribon.

"Uh, no sir. Where can I get one?"

The security guard pointed at a ticket booth just to the left of the entryway. "Are you here with family or a group?"

Charlee thought fast, but no appropriate lie came to her. "No."

"I see. You just decided to come to the museum by yourself on a Saturday morning?"

"Uh-huh."

The security guard's face softened. "Just be sure to get yourself a ticket." With that, he sauntered off.

Charlee walked over to the ticket booth. It was fortunate that the pants she had chosen to wear had a few dollars that had been left in one of the pockets. She had just enough to pay the five-dollar entry fee. Now it was time to figure this out. If Dad hid Theodora's medallion in the museum, which hiding spot would he have picked? In the basement, on the roof or behind a painting were possibilities.

"Where do I start? What if it's not even here?" She approached a digital museum directory. At the top a sign read, "Find it." Underneath was a map of the museum with a star at the entryway. Below the star were the words:

"You are here." Green digital numbers covered the map. At the side of the map, each number had a corresponding gallery name. Her eyes locked on one gallery. The Medieval Gallery on the third floor. That had to be it. After all, didn't her dad teach that stuff? Didn't he drag the family off to a Renaissance faire or two each year where grown men in costumes pretended to fight each other with swords?

Her dad spent hours in the backyard practicing with all types of swords, as if he was some kind of knight. Where did he get all those swords? Her thoughts drifted to the rest of her family and the danger she'd placed them in.

"How could I have been such a fool?" Charlee leaned against the directory and a cracking sound rose from its base, yet another reminder of her strength. "Why didn't Mom and Dad tell me the truth?" she asked softly, backing away from the directory. "I don't even know who I am anymore. If we survive this, we're going to have a long talk."

With heavy strides, she marched to the elevator, passing people happily unaware a powerful sorceress was somewhere in the city ready to turn everyone into her monstrous slaves, or worse—kill everyone. She couldn't let that happen. Not even the bike would be enough to stop Theodora. The medallion was her only hope.

A line of people waited at the glass elevator. Hoping to save time, Charlee chose the spiraling staircase and sprinted up to the third floor.

Once there, she took in the grand scale of the Medieval Gallery, built to resemble the inside of a castle complete with electric torches. The orange light from the illusionary flames shone on suits of armor, colorful shields, and swords of every description. Artwork covered the walls while mannequins dressed in medieval clothing filled sections of the gallery. Some wore fancy, brightly colored robes and others were dressed in drab, torn rags. The mannequins were arranged as though performing daily activities.

"All right medallion, where are you?" She walked to the center of the gallery. Nothing stood out.

She clasped her hands and squeezed her fingers in frustration. While no clues showed themselves, hidden cameras came into focus. Security would be on her instantly if she made any suspicious moves like lifting a painting or worse, smashing through a wall.

Charlee knew she would do whatever it took, even if it meant causing a little damage. Fortunately, only a few people were in the gallery and they wouldn't stop her search. Security was another story.

Her body ached and eyes grew increasingly heavy—both signs strength and energy faded. She needed to touch the bike again, but it would have to wait.

Stepping toward the displays that lined the gallery, she looked for any clues her dad might have left. *Come on! Where are you?* Over her shoulder, she discovered a display case filled with coins and amulets. It would make perfect sense to have placed the medallion among them. Her hopes were quickly crushed. No medallion. A search of the rest of the gallery revealed nothing. She sat down on a bench with fingers covering her eyes and head bowed.

"What am I going to do?" She wiped away a tear.

"A knight does not wallow in self-pity," a familiar voice said.

She smiled at the criticism, sniffing back another tear. "Tribon!"

"Yes."

Charlee lifted her face. The knight wasn't there. "Tribon, where are you?"

"I am very near. Remember, I am in your mind, so I am always with you—watching." His voice emanated from a space beside Charlee.

Charlee seethed. She slung a strand of hair away from her face. "If you're always with me, where have you been? Why haven't you spoken to me?"

"Knights must learn to walk in their own armor."

"What is that supposed to mean?"

"I believe you already know the answer."

"I've run out of ideas. I don't know where to find the medallion and soon I have to face Theodora." The scared girl within her reached out for something—someone—to hold onto. "Tribon, let me open a gateway for you. It must be time."

"You are correct," Tribon agreed. "The time grows near."

"So...now?" Charlee pleaded.

"Almost, my young knight. Almost. Be patient. A mistake now when we are so close could prove disastrous."

"What do you mean?"

"Stay focused. Don't lose faith in yourself. You have the strength of heart to complete your task, and soon I will be there to fight at your side. It will be my honor to do so."

"Tribon!"

"Remember my words." The knight's voice disappeared and Charlee was alone once more. She clenched a fist and pounded the bench. A crack rang through the gallery as the wood split.

Visitors eyed her and moved with haste from the gallery. *Brilliant, butthead!* She reached down to pick up a piece of the splintered wood and something strange caught her eye.

Across the gallery, a rounded object hung from the neck of a finely-dressed mannequin. It was almost invisible against the deep black cloak. Maybe that's why she had missed it the first time. The object swallowed any light that tried to bounce off it. This strange effect caused the medallion to disappear within the cloak's darkness. *Could it be?* Charlee rose, rubbing her eyes. The medallion! Was it real? It had to be. But why had she not felt its presence. If it was so powerful, shouldn't she sense it?

"Maybe I was just too focused on my little pity party," she told herself because now she was drawn to it, whether by some magical force or by her own desire to use its power.

Charlee approached it, sweat forming over her brow, legs wobbling. The closer she got, the tougher each step became. As bad as she wanted the medallion, the ache radiating from deep in her stomach warned her of danger. The vision of her warped face returned. If she touched it, would she begin a decent into evil, like Theodora? Her legs became rooted to the ground as if unwilling to take another step.

"You can't stop now," she told herself. "You need the medallion no matter how it changes you."

Charlee's body shook as she willed hers muscles to respond. "Do it now!" she urged. "There's no time." She would just have to withstand any poisonous influence from the medallion long enough to stop Theodora. After that, she'd have to find a way to destroy it before it destroyed her. Exhaling a lungful of air, Charlee took one more lumbering step toward the medallion and another.

When she stood within an arm's length, her whole body tingled. It might be one more danger signal, but it didn't matter. Another thought took over. *Take it and you'll become a conqueror.*

Charlee blinked. "Where did that come from? Forget it. Stay calm. You're still in control. Remember that."

Licking her dry lips, she ducked under the rope and glided to the object. Just like her vision, it was just a bit larger than her hand—a rounded stone of some kind as black as a raven's features. It had to be the medallion. With jittery hands, she reached out to lift it from the mannequin's neck. As her hands grew closer, an icy sensation rose up her fingers, snaked up shaking arms to her shoulders. Charlee recoiled.

"It's too late to be a chicken."

Rubbing away the numbness, she reached for the necklace again, ignoring the chill that crept up her back.

"Come on…almost there." Her fingers were inches away.

With one more breath, her fingers bridged the last few inches and made contact. The cool, smooth piece of chiseled stone lay heavy in her hands. Grasping it tightly, she closed her eyes. Any second, a burst of energy would likely knock her down, but the object imparted no strange sensation. Charlee held it with both hands for several more moments, but still nothing happened.

"Is this the medallion?" she questioned. "Shouldn't something, anything be happening?"

Attached to the medallion was a thick band made of tarnished gold strands interwoven to form a necklace. She lifted the golden band from the mannequin's neck and found only clips attached it to the medallion. Removing those, the golden band dropped to the floor.

Charlee brought the medallion close to her face, trying to compare it with the vision she had of the mysterious object. One side had the image of a burning tree, but what about the other side. Would her face be there? Flipping the medallion over, she relaxed for the first time in two days. No engraving of her face marred the medallion. This side had no markings at all. Perhaps her fate had not yet been written. Perhaps there was a way to defeat Theodora without becoming infected by evil.

A voice inside—that same one she had heard before, a voice that did not seem to be her own or Tribon's—told her it was the true medallion. But could she trust the voice?

From somewhere in the gallery whispers grabbed her attention. She had lingered too long. It was time to get out, get back to the bike, open a gateway for Tribon, and figure out how to use the medallion to stop Theodora. The time had come to go save the city—to save the world.

"I'll be taking that, little girl."

Charlee froze.

Chapter 22

The Cooler

O ver Charlee's shoulder, the burly security guard she had first spoken with in the museum lobby stood. She thought about tackling him like a football player but there had to be another way than hurting him for doing his job. That is if she had enough strength to overcome a man three times her size. The bike's energy was quickly draining from her limbs. Arm muscles that had felt so strong moments ago were growing mushy.

Running wasn't much of an option either. More security officers approached and soon blocked any escape route. Cornered! What about trying the truth? No, they wouldn't believe her. Fighting her way out seemed like the only option, but she couldn't bring herself to strike them. She pictured the image of her aged face on the medallion. A hero wouldn't hurt the innocent.

Bowing her head, she handed over the medallion to the burly guard. She would wait for the right moment, grab the medallion, and then escape. The bike would help. It was always there. *Bike! I need you…again,* Charlee called out with her thoughts.

The security guards led her from the gallery to a main hallway along the third floor. They passed visitors to the museum who stared and whispered. Charlee's face burned with embarrassment as she was paraded through the museum like a criminal. Thankfully, they guided her to a service elevator for museum staff away from the public. It was a long ride down beyond the first floor to the basement.

When the elevators doors opened, the guards directed her along a sterile hallway with white walls unadorned by any of the lavish artwork and artifacts that filled the floors above. The clip clop of their shoes on the tiled floor was the only sound as no one spoke to her until they reached the security office.

Pushing open double doors, the security guard who called her a *little girl—* who must be the supervisor of this pack—pointed for Charlee to sit at a conference table. As she followed his orders, she did a quick survey of the office. They were in a main room, about as big as her living room with portable

113

dividers to separate the guards' work areas. To the right was a side office where one guard sat with his eyes fixed on security monitors. In the back of the main room was another set of double doors with a sign above that read, *Cooler.*

"What we're going to do is contact your parents and have them come down here to pick you up," the supervisor said as Charlee sat at the table.

"You can't do that," she protested.

"I'm sorry, but there have to be consequences." He shook his head, his hands resting on his large stomach. "I knew you were trouble when I saw you in the lobby. All I want to do is get your parents here and resolve this matter."

"You're not going to be able to reach my parents right now." Charlee raised her voice, her eyes shifting among the guards. "They won't be home."

"Don't make this difficult. If you do, we'll have no other recourse than to contact the authorities. Is that what you want?" The supervisor leaned in close and Charlee smelled bacon on his breath. "Just work with me and we can get this straightened out. Why don't you give me a cell number to your parents?"

"You don't understand." Charlee stood.

"Sit down. Now!" he commanded. "One more time, will you cooperate with us? All we want to do is send you off with your parents and let them decide on your punishment."

This time she was silent.

The supervising security guard shook his head. Keeping his eyes on Charlee, he motioned to the two other guards. "Call the police. Tell them we caught a thief who won't cooperate. Place her in the cooler for now."

"Please, you have to listen to me!" Charlee jumped to her feet. "There's a lot at—"

"Little girl, whatever you're going to say, you should have thought about it before you decided to break the law. Now, I have a museum to watch over. We'll let the police decide what to do with you." The supervisor nodded to the two guards. "One of you, stay here with this kid. She's trouble. Contact me when the police arrive. I'm going to inform the curator about our little thief."

Charlee watched as the supervisor, with her medallion in hand, marched from the office followed by one of the guards. What now? Was it time to knock the security guards out with whatever strength remained, snatch the medallion back and make a run for it?

"All right, kid," the remaining guard smirked. "Get up. You heard the man. You're going in the cooler for a while."

The cooler?

He grabbed Charlee's arm and led her through the double doors in the back of the security office. On the other side was a barren room with nothing inside but a holding cell—a steel cage the size of a closet. The cooler! Things were not going well. She entered the cage and slumped as the door slammed shut. No, things were not going well at all.

When the guard disappeared through the double doors, Charlee grasped the steel bars. Did the icy sensation she felt come from the bars or from her own sense of failure? Perhaps she had already allowed Theodora to win. Maybe she wanted to give up, and that's why she allowed herself to be caught so easily.

Perhaps she was just tired. No! She pounded her fists against the bars.

§ § §

Charlee wasn't sure how long she stayed in the cell, weighing her options. It could have been minutes, but it felt a lot longer.

While she searched for an answer, that soft voice returned to ease her worries. *Everything will work out. You just have to trust in yourself.*

"Who are you? Who's in my head? Tribon is that you? Bike? Speak to me." Charlee stood, heart hammering in her chest, but the voice went quiet. "Well, that's just great."

She paced the cell. One option danced in her mind—open a gateway. But what would that mean? If she opened a gateway to try to escape, would she be able to control where the gateway led? Would she still be able to open another one for Tribon or would she lose any hope of bringing the giant knight across?

Then again, she could bring Tribon to the museum so that he could bust her out of this tiny jail but chances were the knight would be so disappointed that the *Last Guardian* had not been able to free herself.

Tribon had said it was not yet time and there could be danger in bringing him to this world too early. She had to trust him.

"All right, that's it," she decided. "I'm breaking myself out of here. I'll fight my way out. I have no other choice." Charlee didn't care if the security guards watched her through the cameras overhead.

"Let's do this." She grabbed the cell door, gritted her teeth, and prepared to bust through to freedom. She counted down from three to one and pushed but nothing happened. She tried again, straining against the bars. Still nothing. She wasn't ready to give up. Taking three steps back, Charlee threw herself against the door. She crashed hard but the steel bars remained unbroken.

"Hey, knock it off in there," the guard who placed her in the cell ordered through speakers likely hidden in the ceiling. "Just calm down. The police will be here soon. If you think you're going to escape, forget about it. You've dug your own grave on this one, kid."

"You're telling me." She slumped back onto the bench. "Great. My strength is gone." To make matters worse, her vision was blurring—another sign that the powers faded. "I need you, bike, but how can you reach—"

From the other room came the sound of chairs shuffling. Charlee strained to hear what was happening. Fortunately, she still had a bit of her super hearing.

"You let a bird into the office?" one of the guards complained.

"I didn't know it was a bird—I heard a tapping at the door." Charlee recognized this second speaker as the guard who placed her in the cell.

"Well, get rid of it," said the other man.

"What—are you scared of a little—"

At that moment a white bird—maybe a pigeon but more like a dove—burst through the double doors and circled over the holding cell.

Charlee fell back onto the bench, eyes wide. How could a bird force its way through the doors?

The answer came quickly as the dove hovered in front of her and began to transform. Its body grew, bent, and twisted.

"What the…?" Before Charlee finished the thought, handles burst from the bird's head and the beak disappeared. The bird's two eyes became one and altered to become a reflector. In another heartbeat the metamorphosis ended.

The bike was before her.

Chapter 23

Let Me Out!

Charlee charged the cell door. "Bike! How?" She shook her head. "Never mind, stupid question. No time. We've got to get out of here. I've lost my strength. You've got to bust me out."

"No one's busting anyone out of anywhere," a familiar voice countered.

"Mr. Flores!" Charlee tried to push her face through the steel bars.

Sandra's dad, accompanied by two of his officers, stood in the small room just outside the cell. "Quiet," the deputy chief ordered. "Like I said, no one is busting you out of here. Not yet, anyway." He looked tired—as though he had slept about as much as she had. His uniform was tattered and dirty, the sleeves frayed. He glared at the security guards. "Who is in charge here?"

"I am, sir," said the supervisor, now back in the room. "I caught this young lady stealing this item from our Medieval Gallery." He held up the medallion.

"And you thought the offense warranted a call to police?" asked Mr. Flores, raising a brow.

"Well, I...we gave her a chance to contact her parents, but she refused, so we had no choice but to contact the police. She's a criminal. She tried to take a valuable museum piece and, well, the curator wants to press charges."

"I see." Mr. Flores rubbed his chin. "Would you mind giving me that piece as evidence? I can assure you the Police Department will take special care of it."

The supervisor handed the medallion to Mr. Flores. While it changed hands, Charlee reached her arm through the bars of the cell, trying to touch the bike. If she could touch it just once, perhaps some of its power would jump to her. She needed the powers back...now.

"Don't even think about it." Mr. Flores directed his command at her. He held the medallion close to his face as if to study it but kept his eyes on her.

"Yes, sir," Charlee spoke softly, more a scared schoolgirl than a potential hero. "But the time—"

"I'm aware of the time." Mr. Flores nodded to the two police officers who had come with him. "I need everyone out of this room. I don't want anyone on this floor. Take up positions outside the security office."

He turned to the supervising security guard. "I appreciate your efforts in this case. I need some time alone to question this girl. Please return to your duties upstairs."

The supervisor and the other guards reluctantly complied as they were led out by Mr. Flores' officers.

"Wait," Mr. Flores called after them. "I need the key to the cell."

Soon everyone was gone except Charlee, the bike and Mr. Flores. "All right, I need answers." He inserted the key into the cell door and swung it open. "I need to know why my jail is filled with those creatures you say are humans. Every hour we pick up more of those…things. I need to know what we're dealing with and how to fix it before panic breaks out." He paused. "And believe me, panic is just a few short hours away."

Charlee gulped. "Mr. Flores, there's no—"

"Answers, now!"

Charlee stared into Mr. Flores' dark eyes. They were Sandra's eyes—just as intense, just as deep. There was nothing left but to tell the man what he wanted to know, whether he would believe it or not.

"All right," she lamented. "You want to know what's going on, I'll tell you. But when I'm done, you have to let me go. Everything depends on me getting out of here with that medallion you're holding."

"We'll see."

"It started with a dream about some princess and a giant knight," Charlee began. She then unfolded the story of how the sorceress Theodora had tricked her into opening a gateway to Earth to seek out the medallion he now held and how the bike had magical powers and for some reason had come into her life. Charlee explained how she was part of a bloodline of guardians and was the only one who could stop Theodora. She finished with the sorceress' threat to enslave everyone—the entire world—if she didn't get her medallion by tonight.

Charlee then waited for his reaction. None came.

"Mr. Flores?"

"Quiet." The deputy chief gently tapped his forehead with a fist. "I'm trying to think. This whole thing stinks, and I have a banging headache."

Charlee did not dare speak further, not sure what to expect from the man who looked like he was about to explode. That's just what happened. He pounded both fists on the table and flung a chair against a wall, his chest heaving rapidly. Charlee flinched and covered her head with her hands.

Finally he spoke. "All right, kid. I've seen things in the last few hours I can't explain—things I know will haunt my dreams forever. Right now, I have no choice but to believe you. Basically, kid, I have no choice but to entrust the safety of the city to you. Are you up to the challenge?"

"Yes, sir." Charlee raised her head. "I guess I have to be. I'm the only one who can stop her."

"That may be the case, but there's no way I'm letting you out of my sight. I'm now your full-time bodyguard."

Charlee nearly smiled. Mr. Flores sounded so much like his daughter. There was no point in arguing with the deputy chief, but she could not let Sandra's dad risk his life. She would wait until the right time to ditch him. For now, she would accept Mr. Flores' offer.

"Mr. Flores, thank you for believing in me."

"Don't thank me. I have no choice. I have a city to protect. Do you understand?"

She nodded. "Uh, one more thing…can you please give me back the medallion?"

He hesitated then tossed it to her the way he would toss a Frisbee. Charlee caught it with two hands and held it against her chest. She would never let it go again. It was hers now and she would find a way to tap into its power to stop Theodora or anyone who crossed her.

"That's not right," she whispered. "It's not mine—I don't even want it. I just want to stop Theodora and destroy it." Charlee pried the medallion away from her chest, but her arms hugged it tightly against her body again. What was she doing? She had to maintain control, but how long until the medallion's corrupting influence took over.

"Kid, what are you saying?" Mr. Flores stepped toward her. "Are you all right? You just turned white as a ghost."

"I'm fine." She lowered the medallion, holding it tucked under her right arm.

"Then let's show this sorceress of yours just what our city is made of." The deputy chief wrapped an arm around Charlee's shoulders and the two were about to head out of the security office when the ring of Mr. Flores' cell phone stopped them. Even before he answered Charlee sensed a problem. It had something to do with Sandra.

"Baby, slow down. I can't understand. Taken? Letter? How? When?" Mr. Flores removed his arm from Charlee and paced back and forth. "Baby, I'm on my way. I'll get a unit dispatched there immediately. We'll deal with this.

She'll be all right. Whoever took her will pay. I'll make sure of that. But first we've got to find her. I promise you we will. Baby, hold on!"

Mr. Flores tapped a button on his cell. "All units, this is Deputy Chief Flores. My daughter has been kidnapped. I need any available units to meet me at my residence. Fifteen minutes. I need an APB alert, too. I want every jurisdiction within a hundred miles on lookout. Flores, out."

Charlee's fists tightened. This had to be the work of Theodora. She would pay. "It's Theodora. I'm sorry."

"If my daughter is hurt in any way, I hold you responsible."

"I already hold myself responsible." Charlee gazed up at Mr. Flores.

Mr. Flores stared back at her. "All right, my car's outside. We're going to make a stop at my house and see about this letter. Then we'll take down Theodora and get my daughter back." He grabbed Charlee's arm and started to lead her out of the room.

Charlee ripped her arm away. "Forget your car!"

"What do you mean?"

She pointed to the bike. "I've got a better way."

§ § §

"Hold on," Charlee directed when Mr. Flores had climbed onto the bike behind her.

"Just go!"

"Bike, fly!" With a thrust of its great white wings, the bike launched skyward. Charlee, one hand on the handlebars, the other holding the medallion pressed against her stomach, peered back once at the deputy chief. He kept his eyes fixed forward. He didn't blink. She tried to read the look on his face. The pain he must be feeling and it was because of her.

The bike reached Mr. Flores' home just before fifteen squad cars, their sirens blaring, came to a screeching halt in front of the house. Five unmarked units drove up behind them.

A tall, balding man climbed out of an unmarked sedan and approached the deputy police chief. "Pete, I'm sorry. We're going to find her. I'll put every officer I have on this."

Mr. Flores shook the man's hand. "I appreciate that, Stan."

Charlee assumed the other man was the police chief.

"Pete, the department's at your discretion," the chief said to Mr. Flores. "Tell us how you want to play it."

Mr. Flores nodded. Then he turned to the officers gathered around their units. "I want a perimeter around the house. Right now! Stop anyone who looks suspicious."

An officer with four stripes on his sleeve spoke to the others. "All right, form up. Perimeter enforcement, now. I want two officers each at the front and rear entries of the house. Move!"

Without another word, Mr. Flores ran to the front door of his house. Charlee started to follow, but an officer grabbed her.

"She's with me. Let her go," Mr. Flores directed.

The officer frowned at Charlee then released his grip.

"Oh, Peter, they've taken her!" Mrs. Flores cried rising from a chair at the entryway of the house as her husband flung open the door. She collapsed into his arms.

Mr. Flores held his wife tightly. "Who, baby?"

"I...I...I don't know. There was a knock at the door. I answered and then everything went dark. I don't know what they did to me, but when I woke up, she was gone. They left a note. I don't understand. It doesn't make any sense. It says something about a medallion...about returning someone's immortality. Why did they take our daughter, Peter? Why? Find her! Please, you have to find her."

Charlee cursed under her breath. She had to stop Theodora and she had to stop her now. The medallion in her hands was the way to do it, but when would she feel its power? When would she understand how to use it? What if it wasn't the medallion? All would be lost. Tonight, Theodora would begin her assault.

"Mr. Flores, we need to see that note."

Mr. Flores whipped around, his eyes bulging. Charlee understood the silent message and backed away.

"Who is this?" Mrs. Flores asked.

"Uh, no one. She's just a friend of Sands. She's right, baby. We need to see the note."

Mrs. Flores stared at Charlee, fury mixed with terror in her eyes. "You're the one, aren't you?"

Charlee took a step back.

"Baby?" Mr. Flores asked.

"You're the one responsible for this. Aren't you? Answer me." Mrs. Flores grabbed Charlee's shoulders when she did not respond.

"Baby." Mr. Flores took his wife's hands. "Calm—"

"Peter, she's the one in the note. She's the one responsible, isn't she? You know, don't you? You know!"

Mr. Flores pried his wife off Charlee and cradled her in his arms. He led her into the house.

Slowly, Charlee followed. Mrs. Flores was right. She was responsible and now she had to make it right.

The first step was to read the note. Inside the house, two officers armed with rifles took positions at the front door. Charlee took no comfort in their presence. If Theodora wanted to return, she would have no trouble transforming them into her slaves. She forced the thought aside and walked into the living room. There were no signs of struggle.

At the far end of the living room was the entryway into the kitchen. Mr. Flores was already there with his wife, reading the message from Theodora out loud. Charlee approached and stopped at the doorway to listen.

His voice was raspy and desperate; Mr. Flores stopped and choked back tears before continuing.

When he finished, he threw the letter on the kitchen table and stared at Charlee. "This empress of yours is a real piece of work. I'm going to bring that woman down for what she's done to my family and this city. And if she has hurt my daughter…"

"Sir, do you mind if I see the note?" Charlee asked.

"You have to read it. It was written for you…guardian."

Charlee, still clutching the medallion, picked up the note. It was written in red ink on the back of a math worksheet from school. Crimson streaks smudged the edges of the paper as if ink—or blood—had spilled. Charlee started to read.

Young guardian, I fervently hope that as you are reading this, you have in your possession that which is rightfully mine. Now I command you to return it to me and thus fulfill your oath. For good measure, I have taken someone who means a great deal to you.

She paused to rub her red eyes then continued.

If you have failed in your quest, or if you choose to cross me, this fine young girl with such a fiery spirit will serve at my side for eternity. I think I shall make her my daughter, and together we will rule this world. Or shall I just kill her? That would be the easiest after all. Return my medallion! Return my immortality and she will be unharmed. Cross me and her fate will be your doing. I will await you where the castle sits atop water.

Charlee crumbled the note and threw it. "More riddles! Why the riddles?

I have the medallion. She must know that. Why doesn't she just face me? You hear me, Theodora? No more games. Come and get me. I have your medallion." She lifted the medallion over her head. "It's yours for the taking. Just bring Sandra back."

"Don't waste your breath," Mr. Flores uttered. "This...woman...is not going to face you here. She probably fears your power more than you know. Or maybe she can't track you as well as you think she can. I don't know. Maybe her powers are not as strong as she pretends. What I do know is that she's going to set a trap for you—and my daughter is the bait."

Mr. Flores paused and placed a hand on her shoulder. "It's up to you to set your own trap."

In that moment, Charlee formed a plan but to make it work, she would have to figure out Theodora's riddle. That part proved easy. Just as Sandra had done, Mr. Flores provided the answer. "One thing is for sure. This Theodora has picked the perfect spot for a showdown."

"What do you mean?"

"Alcatraz."

"Are you sure?"

Mr. Flores glowered at her. "What other castle sits on water. Alcatraz is not quite a castle, but I could see it being mistaken for one."

"Fine. I'll face her there."

"Kid, we'll face her there. This is my daughter we're talking about. It may be your show, but I have some of my own justice to hand down. I'm going with you."

Charlee nodded.

"Now, guardian, tell me you have a plan."

"I think I do."

"Tell me."

"First I need you to trust me."

"I've already told you, I have no other choice."

"We'll need some supplies—some black paint, some thick tape and something I can use to tie the medallion around my neck."

For now, she would work with Mr. Flores but she would have to find a way to face Theodora alone—when the time was right.

Charlee took a hesitant step to Mrs. Flores. "You're right, this is my fault. But I will bring Sandra back. I promise!"

Chapter 24

The Island Castle

As nightfall blanketed the Bay, Charlee gazed from the pier toward Alcatraz. In daytime, the abandoned penitentiary sitting atop an island was foreboding enough with its sorrowful prison walls where criminals once served their time. Many died, their souls forever trapped inside. Charlee and her family had toured the prison once and she remembered that icy chill up her back as they walked down the abandoned cell blocks. She imagined the ghosts staring at her through the rusted bars of each isolated room.

At night, as lights strewn across the island cast a menacing orange glow over the prison, that chilly feeling of dread worsened. After the tour, she had vowed to never look toward the island again. Now, Theodora had chosen Alcatraz for what could be their final showdown. The sorceress had chosen the prison for a reason. Maybe it reminded her of a fortress back home. Maybe she sensed evil there.

Charlee shivered. She didn't have to face Theodora tonight. She could run away and hide and forget all about the sorceress and Tribon. After all, she was just a teenage girl, not some guardian.

"No, I have to do this." She quietly mouthed as she touched the medallion hanging around her neck by a thin cord. "I can't chicken out. All those people Theodora turned into those beasts need me. Sandra needs me."

Mr. Flores stood next to her. "All right, kid, you ready for this?"

Charlee narrowed her eyes. "I'm sorry."

"For wha—"

With the super strength granted her by the bike, she slugged Mr. Flores in the face, knocking him unconscious. What else could she do? She had to square off against Theodora without him. It was bad enough Sandra was in danger. Mr. Flores would just make the situation more dangerous for everyone. She stared at the deputy chief as he lay on the pier. "Please forgive me." Then Charlee declared to the bike, "Let's fly."

Soaring into the sky, her thoughts turned to Tribon. She wished she could call out for him. Would he be there to help?

She needed the giant knight. Surely, he understood this?

As she and the bike neared Alcatraz, she rolled her shoulders against the weight of the medallion. A heaviness pressed through her skin into the muscle between her shoulder blades. Each breath was labored as if her chest could barely move. It was as if the medallion was sucking away all the energy the bike gave her. At the same time, there was an exhilaration that came from having the medallion so close. Charlee still had no idea how to use it. All she knew is she wanted to unleash its power.

"That's the problem," she reminded herself. "I want the medallion's power too much. If I use it, I know I'll change."

Charlee mentally grappled with the urge to look at the medallion. What if her face was now etched into it? No, it was better not to see that yet—better not to know her fate. She was still in control and had to keep it that way.

Gripping the handlebars, Charlee concentrated on the island. The Rock, as the island was called, loomed ahead, the orange glow of florescent lights causing shadows to dance off the prison houses. "Bike, let's circle it once or twice."

Alcatraz was a massive construction of formidable walls clearly meant to break the spirit of any inmate. The entire island from its buildings, to a water tower and lighthouse seemed a place of sadness—a place where someone like Theodora would thrive.

As the bike completed one circuit around the prison, Charlee searched for Sandra and the sorceress. Phantom movements, more illusionary than real, were all that she could see, but Theodora was close—there was little doubt of that. She had the same sensation as in her first encounter with the sorceress atop the skyscraper—like she was going to die...alone. It made her stomach ache. Even with the bike with her, the feeling was inescapable as if Theodora had cast a spell to weaken her resolve. Oh yes, Theodora was close.

Charlee sent an urgent thought to Tribon. *Look, if you're going to help me, now is the time. I'm sorry to be a wimp, but I'm afraid. I don't want to die. I'm not strong enough to be a guardian, but I'll try no matter what happens.*

"That's the spirit," the now familiar voice responded, carried on the wind.

"Tribon?"

"Yes. I am with you, young guardian. You are ready to open a gateway. But do so when you know that the time is right."

"The time is right now."

126

"No. Concentrate. Think with a warrior's cunning. Think of surprising your enemy. Catch the enemy off guard. Then destroy her."

"Right," Charlee agreed. "Take us in, bike," Charlee instructed, emboldened by Tribon. The bike landed on the far side of the island, just beyond the prison walls and away from the hazy lighting. Charlee climbed off and paced in a slow circle around her winged friend, trying to control her panting breaths and drumming heart. The moon cast its own pale light over the prison grounds, but that just added to the mysterious manifestations that seemed to leap at her.

Charlee trudged farther from the bike, tightening her hands into fists to keep them from shaking. "Come on out, Theodora! I know you're here." Her voice quivered. "I've got the medallion. Now let Sandra go. This is between you and me."

Silence reigned over the island.

"Theodora!" Charlee bellowed. "Are you afraid?"

"GRRR!"

From the walls above, a beast pounced landing hard on Charlee's back. As she fell to the ground, the creature sunk its fangs into her shoulder, tearing through flesh. Warm blood splattered onto her neck and face. The creature twisted its snout back and forth, biting deeper into muscle. Searing heat rose from the creature's snout, boiling her skin.

Charlee cried out as she thrashed her arms and kicked her legs, but the beast had her pinned. As it lifted its head from her shoulder, Charlee got her first glimpse of the predator. It was one of the unfortunate victims Theodora transformed into her half human, half wolf slaves. Drool dripped from bloody fangs but it was a woman's face, warped and elongated as if only half way through the mutation. A low snarl rose from the beast's throat.

The she wolf arched her back and spewed a painful shriek into the night. Charlee desperately wanted to cover her ears, but the woman held her down. Lifting a clawed hand with skin bubbling and popping through the transformation, the woman was about to slice Charlee across the face.

"Bike—"

From over the beast's shoulder, a huge white wing swiped at its head. With a yelp, the morphed woman was knocked off Charlee. She rolled along the ground until she lay still, whimpering like a wounded animal.

Through the haziness of her pain, Charlee lifted herself. The bike stood beside her. "You saved me again," she stuttered, forcing air in and out of her lungs and cradling her hurt shoulder. Smoke rose from the wound. Blood spread through torn flesh and her ripped shirt. She tried to vomit but nothing came.

Gripping the bike's handlebars, Charlee absorbed as much energy as she could. She cried out as an electric shock pulsed through her arm causing the shredded flesh around her shoulder to stretch and reattach to muscle. The healing had begun, but she couldn't linger in the moment. Releasing the bike, she lumbered toward the woman and knelt down to her.

"Are you all right?" Charlee cringed through the pain as her muscles and tissues continued to reconnect. "Can you understand me?"

She placed a hand on the woman's furry shoulder. Staring at Charlee with scared yellow eyes, the woman tried to speak.

"Help me..."

Before the woman could finish, the wolf in her took control and with a growl she lunged at Charlee.

The bike again slapped the creature. She crumbled to the ground and slunk off into the night.

Charlee painfully climbed to her feet. Even with the help of the bike, an icy chill weakened her knees, and she just wanted to slump to the ground—to sleep.

"You can't," she told herself, placing a hand on the medallion around her neck to make sure it was still there. She couldn't give up like this. "Remember Sandra. Think of that poor woman." She held the medallion tightly in both hands. "You have to fight. Don't let Theodora win this easily."

The bike nudged her leg and she reached for the frame. Charlee stood a little taller as her limbs strengthened and muscles tightened. Her shoulder ached, but the skin had fully reformed. "Thanks, bike. I think I'm—"

Pained, inhuman breathing interrupted her. Steps sounded from behind. Charlee swung around. Another of Theodora's wolves charged her. She turned away as a long claw cleaved through her left side just above the waist.

This time though Charlee didn't give in to the stinging wound and blood that poured from it. She turned and rushed at the monster, striking at it wildly with clenched fists.

The creature fell to the ground. Charlee jumped on top and grabbed its neck, preparing to deliver a last punch. But as she stared into the beast's face, the snout disappeared and the yellow eyes vanished. A young man's appearance replaced the wolf snout. His eyes were dazed, mouth agape. "What's happening...to me," he asked, his voice shaky.

Charlee kept hold of the man's neck but eased her grip. Although his human face had returned, from the neck down his body remained...wolf-like.

"Please don't hurt me," the man pleaded. Then he convulsed and let out a howl before disappearing—as if he had never been there. Charlee patted the ground and whirled around but saw no sign of him.

"How did he do that?"

Charlee slowly stood, hands clutching the gashes on her side. Blood seeped from each cut. She needed to touch the bike once again, needed to feel its energy course through her.

"Why did you let this happen?" The words came from in front of her. She did not recognize the voice.

A second unfamiliar voice spoke. "We are suffering. Why don't you help us?"

A third joined in. "You failed us."

Three twisted creatures in different stages of their transformation magically appeared. One had a woman's face and a wolf's body. Another had an animal head and human body. The third, a man, was fully human except for his fangs, claws and yellow eyes. All three stood between her and the bike. More of the monsters approached, some walking upright, some on all fours, while others were hunched over and limping. Their skin sizzled and popped. Blood dripped from eyes, like tears, and backbones arched and tore through flesh. Some were completely covered in fur. Others seemed to be itching away their own skin as the fur still spread.

The creatures surrounded her, chanting, "You failed. You failed. You failed!"

"I'm sorry!" Charlee cried.

But the chanting continued.

Charlee closed her eyes and covered her ears. "I didn't mean for this to happen. I tried to stop her from hurting you. I can fix this. Give me a chance." Pictures played through her mind of all the people in her life. Her mother, father, Megan, Sandra—they all chanted her failure with anger in their faces.

Even the bully Tina Lomeli appeared to her. "You're no hero, Chub. You're a loser."

"No," Charlee screamed, shaking her head. Then the chanting both around her and inside her head faded. When she opened her eyes, the creatures were gone, the prison grounds quiet, but her face burned with the shame of all the people she had let down.

"Theodora's twisting my mind. It's all part of her game. Don't listen. Be strong. Be strong! Theodora, how many of these creatures are going to fight me? Face me yourself—or are you scared?"

A rumbling rose from inside the island and the ground shook violently. Charlee stumbled as the rocky terrain off to the right collapsed, causing a sinkhole that could swallow a car. "Bike, get away," she shouted. Finding her balance, Charlee ran, covering her ears from the land's deafening roar. A thunderous explosion stopped her. Steam surged from the hole followed by a gurgling as if the island was choking.

Then came the lava.

"What? How" That was impossible. This was an island, not an active volcano. Charlee eyed the bike as if it could provide an answer. "What's happening?"

The lava glowed bright red and crackled as it flowed from the hole like her own blood leaked from her wounds. A wave of heat baked the island and the glow coated the prison in a crimson mist.

Charlee reached for the bike. "Let's fly!"

A second explosion threw Charlee to her back. When she looked up, the lava gushed into the sky like a geyser. At its peak, the flow formed into an unnatural shape.

"Oh no, a hand!" Her eyes fixed on the giant fiery fingers that hovered overhead. "Theodora, stop this. I've brought the medallion."

The sorceress offered no response. Instead, the blazing hand reached for her. Charlee dove to the ground but the fingers grazed her head. She shrieked. Then it was over—the lava gone, the red haze over the island dissipated but the scent of burning sulfur lingered.

Fighting nausea, Charlee staggered to her feet. She stood on unsteady legs and shook a fist toward the sky. "I'm sick of this. Bike, it's our turn. Let's get her." She swung toward her special two-wheeler and wailed.

The bike lay against a rock, its charred wings limp at its side. Smoke rose from the blistered and blackened frame.

"Bike! No!"

Charlee raced over to the bike—her guardian—and tried to touch the handlebars. They were too hot. If it was a living creature—and she believed it was—it had been badly hurt. Dropping to her knees, Charlee wept. "Bike, I'm sorry. Stay with me. I need you." The bike lay motionless.

Pounding the dirt, she shot to her feet. "Show yourself, Theodora! Show me Sandra!"

"In time."

Charlee reached inside her torn, blood-stained shirt and felt the medallion. "Look, Theodora. Here's your medallion. Here's your immortality. Come and take it. Let Sandra go, and then leave."

"Not just...yet," Theodora purred.

"Why? I did what you asked. I'm giving it back to you. You've won. It's over."

"Oh, you will return what is mine. Of that there is no doubt."

"Why don't you show yourself, Aunty Theodora?" Charlee tried to match the sorceress' mocking tone. Tears burned her eyes. "Are you afraid of my power?"

"You have no power that can stand against me, child. Look at yourself. You can barely walk. I have destroyed the winged one, the only weapon you had. You have nothing else. Now the only way you can save your friend and your family—the only way you can save this world—is to return the medallion and join me. Become my slave! If you do not, all that you know will be destroyed."

Charlee stared down at the bike. Grief would have to wait. "I'm not a slave. I will never join you, Empress Theodora."

"Then feel my power!"

Theodora materialized before Charlee. The sorceress appeared young, her blonde hair flowing across her face and over her shoulders. Her crystal blue eyes blazed and a smile revealed glimmering white teeth reflecting the moonlight.

Sandra knelt at her side, head bowed. For a brief moment, she struggled to look up. Her usually sharp eyes were gray, empty—almost soulless. Dirty streaks covered her face. They had to be the remnants of tears. A blood-stained cut marked her right cheek. Sandra's upper lip was split.

"Oh, Sandra." Charlee glanced away. What had Theodora done to her friend? "Why didn't I protect you? I should have been there."

Sandra reached a shaky hand out toward Charlee but quickly lowered it. Her head dropped again to her chest.

Charlee bolted to Sandra but slammed into an invisible wall. Momentarily knocked off her feet, she rose and struck the barrier. "No, Sandra. I'm coming." She pounded the wall again, tried to get around it, but it was no use.

Backing away, Charlee rubbed her throbbing hands together. "Theodora, what have you done?"

"Nothing worse than I shall do to you, guardian."

"Do it! I'm ready for you this time."

Theodora raised her hands over her head and uttered an incantation. A smoldering ball grew from her fingertips, its red glow consuming her face, twisting her appearance.

This was it. The battle for Sandra, for her family, the city, even the world, was upon her. If what Tribon had said was true, she was a guardian, which meant that perhaps her whole life had been leading to this moment and ready or not she had to face it. It was just her and Theodora, her great-aunt.

One would not survive the night. Charlee willed strength into her muscles. She pushed fear aside. If she was to make a stand, it had to be now.

Theodora's arm shot forward, hurtling the deadly energy.

"Now," Charlee shouted.

She punched the air with an open hand, hoping she had enough enhanced strength to block the blast. Theodora's magical attack struck, exploded into flames, and then dissipated. Charlee's hand burned as if she had dipped it into boiling water, only ten times worse. The smoke cleared. Despite the searing sensation, her hand was unmarked. She had taken Theodora's worst— at least, she hoped it was the sorceress' worst. That meant Charlee had the power to stand up to Theodora, but for how long?

"Is that all you've got, Theodora? My little sister throws harder than that."

"Child, you will die!"

"Not today."

Theodora hurled more magic at Charlee. One of the sorceress' blazing cannonballs screamed toward her. Just as before, Charlee blocked it with an open hand. It seared her hand, but she ignored the pain and took a step forward, planting her feet to withstand the assault.

Theodora continued, whizzing one wave of magic after another. Charlee blocked them all, pushing forward with each attempt. Each discharge crashed against her palms like tiny explosions. The sounds must have echoed all across the Bay, from the island to the harbor.

"You can't back down," Charlee urged herself. "You must move forward. That's the only way to stop her."

"Does it hurt, girl?" Theodora didn't let up the attack.

Charlee blocked it. "Getting tired, old woman?"

Theodora's assault seemed to be weakening, her magic losing strength. The energy blasts hurt less with each impact. The sorceress' blonde locks faded to gray and her flawless skin cracked and shriveled. Delicate fingers became bony.

If Charlee could get close enough, she could throw one good super punch at the sorceress and end this. She tucked her head, like driving forward against a strong wind, and took the last few steps to reach Theodora.

The magical onslaught stopped. Charlee peered up. Sandra stood directly in front of her, a guard protecting Theodora. Sandra's eyes were wide open. Close up Charlee could see her pupils were now a gray void covered with crimson lines. Her brown skin had turned green as if she were a zombie. Drops of blood fell from her wounds.

Charlee trembled. She wanted to reach for Sandra, to hug her, to make everything all right, but she stood motionless waiting for what would come next.

"Guardian, you have done well," Theodora mused. "Now look into the eyes of my daughter. To get to me, you must kill her."

"Daughter? You're a crazy witch, Theodora. Sandra has a mom and dad, and I'm taking her home." Charlee gently reached out to touch Sandra's shoulder. "Try to remember who you are, Sandra. Try."

Sandra responded by slamming a fist into Charlee's face. The impact sent a shockwave of pain through her worse than any brain freeze she had ever experienced. Charlee toppled to the ground. "Sandra, please! Wake up," she begged.

Clearly under Theodora's spell—one that filled her with strength—Sandra bent down and reached for Charlee's throat.

"Sandra, fight the spell," Charlee pleaded, scrambling to her feet.

Sandra threw another punch. Charlee dodged it but was struck by a third punch to her stomach. A fourth caught her along the cheek, dropping her to her knees. It took longer to steady herself this time, but she had to stand up one more time for herself and her friend.

"What's the matter, Charlee? Are you still afraid to fight, like at school?" It was Sandra who spoke, but it wasn't her voice. This voice was warped, bitter. It was nothing like the kind, sweet voice Charlee knew.

"Theodora, let her go!" Charlee continued to back away from Sandra.

"Why should I? This is so much fun. And I have one more surprise for you."

Charlee backed into a wall, or rather into something large and immovable.

"I am here, young knight."

Chapter 25

How Could You Do It?

Charlee spun around to behold the giant knight.

It was him—Tribon. He stood before her just as he had before in his long black cloak and sword at his side. His bushy red beard rested on his chest. If she wasn't so sore, Charlee would have leaped into the knight's arms. A moment ago she had felt so alone. Now she had a friend.

"Tribon, it's time. I need you. Let me bring you across now. I can't fight Theodora alone."

Tribon tilted his head back and released a bellowing laugh.

"Hold on, you're here now though, aren't you?" Charlee realized, backing away from the knight who had been her mentor.

"You are a smart one." Tribon stepped toward her, his hand on the handle of his sword.

"I don't understand." Charlee blinked. The knight's voice was different—no longer kind.

"I've always been here, young knight."

"What? How? But I thought…?"

"I have been here to prepare you for this day—the day when, like me, you shall join your empress in glorious conquests."

Charlee shook her head. What was he saying? She hastened her retreat.

Theodora strolled over to Tribon and leaned against his hulking body. "Do you recall the day you opened a gateway that brought me to this world, child? I told you then that Tribon was aligned with the empress. I did not lie. I simply withheld that I was his empress. A silly omission, I admit, but no lie."

Charlee glanced from Theodora to Tribon. "All this time, you've been serving Theodora?"

"Yes. I was given a choice, just as you now have." He spoke coldly, no longer as the wise warrior she had come to depend on. Her chest felt empty as if she had just lost a dear friend. How could he betray her? How? Anger crashed through her body like waves pounding the shore. There was no more room for grief or fear—just confusion and hatred. Her face burned, the veins in her forehead throbbed. If she had her own sword, she would have buried it in him.

"I could have died on the battlefield serving your grandfather," Tribon continued, "but I chose to live in the new age that my empress would create. Michala could have joined me, but he was too much of a fool."

The giant knight took another step forward. "Don't be like him. Join us, and you will have anything your heart desires."

Charlee peered at Sandra who stood not far behind Tribon. Somewhere deep inside, Sandra's spirit was struggling to free itself. Tribon was supposed to help save her, but he had chosen Theodora's side long ago. His betrayal stung so much that Charlee's heart ached worse than the gash at her side. The sorceress meant for him to break her spirit. He hadn't. She had to fight on for Sandra, for her family…for all those unfortunate victims of Theodora's twisted magic.

Driven by rage and a renewed resolution to save her friend, Charlee stopped her back pedaling. "Sorry, I'm a guardian, and I can only hope to be half the guardian my grandfather Michala was," Charlee declared. "I figure I better start doing a better job. I think I'll begin by kicking your butt."

The giant knight unsheathed his massive sword. "All right, guardian. You have made your choice." Tribon raised the sword over his head. "Pity, it is time for you to die."

Charlee froze. As if in slow motion, the mass of steel swept down toward her head. Charlee dove to the ground, expecting to feel the sword strike her body, but the blow never came. Rolling over, Charlee fixed her eyes on Tribon, who stood motionless, his sword at his side. Sticking through his chest, directly where his heart should be was a long, sharp spike.

His mouth gaped and eyes bulged. He dropped his sword and tried to pry the spike from his chest. When it wouldn't budge, he wheezed a final breath before his eyes rolled up in his head and body went limp. A second later the spike slid out and Tribon fell to the ground.

Standing behind Tribon's body was a unicorn. It glowed bright white. The beast was ferocious but noble.

Where had this creature come from? Charlee glanced back at the rock where her bike had been. It was no longer there. She understood. The bike and the unicorn were the same. Just like the bike had transformed into a dove and flown into the museum, it had now become a…unicorn. Somehow this being had the ability to change shape.

As if the beast understood her thoughts, it limped to her side. Charlee had no idea what this shape-shifting creature truly was, but it was more than a friend. It was a protector. With a shaky hand, she reached up to pat the unicorn's muscular neck.

"I don't know what to say. I don't even know what to call you. I've called you bike all this time. What should I call you?"

The beast lowered its powerful head and nudged Charlee gently. She smiled. "Well, if you're done resting, we've got more work to do. Theodora is—"

Before she could finish, the great beast unleashed an agonized scream. Tribon was on his feet and had plunged his sword into the unicorn's side.

"You cannot kill me so easily, young knight," Tribon laughed.

With a victorious grunt and magically enhanced brute force, he heaved Charlee's protector into the air.

Theodora did the rest. Using her power, she reached out with magic and snatched the unicorn from mid-air. With one cruel thrust, she tossed the creature far out to sea.

"Bike!" A splash sounded in the distance. Her protector was gone and she was alone again.

Theodora and Tribon's laughter filled the night. Charlee wanted to fall to her knees and just give up. Instead, she turned toward them. "Why do this?"

She pointed at Tribon.

The knight's laughter faded. "Long ago, guardian, I realized that Empress Theodora was the rightful ruler of the Kingdom of Latara, indeed all of the Ten Unified Kingdoms and the entire world of Janasara. Her conquest was inevitable. I had a wife and young son, and I wanted them to live. I wanted us all to have a place at her side in the new world order. To obtain that glory, all I had to give up was my heart."

As the giant spoke, Theodora stretched her arm toward Charlee. In her hand she held a heart. It was Tribon's heart. It still beat, but it was more stone than flesh. Bloodless and shriveled, it seemed forever kept in this unnatural state. Not really alive but not quite dead.

Charlee understood. As long as Theodora magically kept the heart beating, Tribon could not be stopped or killed.

"And what happened to your wife and son?" Charlee walked up close enough to Tribon to feel the steam rising from the wound the unicorn inflicted. "Where are they now?"

Tribon was silent.

Theodora answered. "Sad really. Your grandfather's forces took revenge and reached Tribon's wife and son before I could save them. They were brutally killed. Michala's army beheaded them and burned the bodies."

Tribon remained silent as Theodora spoke. The only sign of emotion came when he lowered his head.

Charlee stared at Theodora. A gleam showed in the sorceress' eyes.

"She's lying to you, can't you see that." Charlee shoved Tribon but he did not budge nor did he raise his weapon against her. "My grandfather's army didn't kill your wife and son. She did. She tricked you just like me. Tribon, can't you see? Can't you?"

"No." Tribon raised his head. "My empress would not mislead me. She is all I have left, and I will serve her to the end." His voice cracked and his face shook. It probably wasn't possible, but tears may have formed.

Charlee withdrew and glanced at Sandra. Her friend stood emotionless, staring off into emptiness. She hoped Sandra had not suffered the same fate as Tribon.

"Why did you take Sandra, Theodora?" Charlee started toward the sorceress but Tribon blocked her path. "I told you I would give you the medallion."

"And what of your soul?" Theodora hissed, her bony fingers extended toward Charlee. "Long ago when the medallion was taken from me, I destroyed your grandfather and all he held dear for his treachery, and I vowed his descendants would forever suffer. From that day forward, I have focused my attention on finding the Last Guardian—you. I knew that if I found you, I could easily manipulate your mind so as to gain entry into the world where Michala chose to hide his offspring."

"You mean my mom."

"Yes, the little brat. Imagine my joy at finding that the child of my sister, Queen Assara, has turned out to be nothing. She is so weak that she allows her child to stand in for her. I laugh at what has become of the descendants of Michala and my sister, his wife—the weakest ruler Latara has ever had."

Theodora glided nearer, and her voice softened as she transformed back into the youthful maiden. "But you child are special. There is still time. You have much power. You could join me, and we could put an end to this useless fighting."

Charlee truly understood Theodora's intentions. She didn't just want the medallion—she wanted Charlee. She wanted the Last Guardian to join her and become evil. The medallion burned the skin underneath her torn shirt. Were dark fires starting to weld her face into it? No. She couldn't let that happen. *I will never be Theodora's fool.*

"Sorry, Aunty—find another slave!"

Chapter 26

The Tides of Battle

M ake her suffer," Theodora commanded Tribon and Sandra. "Bring me my medallion. Then bring me her soul."

Both obeyed. "Yes, my empress."

Sandra advanced. "Sandra, no. Fight it," Charlee begged. "Your friendship means everything to me. Sandra, remember. Remember."

As if the words pricked a hole in the spell, Sandra slowed. A brownish hue washed over her face and color returned to her eyes. Sandra's vacant stare disappeared and her lips quivered in a sign of acknowledgement. To further shatter the spell Charlee reached into her pocket and pulled out Sandra's golden cross pendant.

"Sandra, you left this for me in the park. It was your grandmother's. I know why you left it hanging on the bike. Even though you were angry with me, you still wanted to protect me—because we're friends. Sandra, please try and remember."

"Ch…Charlee," Sandra whispered. It was truly her voice, weak but the same friendly voice of the girl who had introduced herself to Charlee in the cafeteria, who stood up to Tina Lomeli and rescued her from the rooftop battle with Theodora.

"Yes!" Charlee approached and placed the pendant in Sandra's right hand, gently closing her fingers around it. Sandra's icy hands were warmed by the pendant. It may not have had special powers, but the love associated with the pendant was enough to overcome Theodora's evil magic.

Charlee smiled—but she couldn't linger in the moment.

Tribon grew close, his sword pointed at her. "Stupid girl, I take no pleasure in killing you."

"How could you do this?" Charlee demanded, backing away. "I trusted you. My grandfather trusted you. Your wife and son trusted you to do the right thing. Why would you give in so easily to Theodora? You're the reason your family is dead. Can't you see that? You have a chance now to make it right. Fight her."

Tribon stopped and lowered his sword. The twisted grin on his face disappeared, but whatever infiltrated Tribon's mind, whatever memory or regret, faded just as quickly. The eerie smirk returned, sword once again ready to strike.

"We all make our choices. I tried to warn Michala, but he would not listen. In the end, not even the Dragon Lord would join his cause and Michala died a pathetic death. He watched as his wife died in a magic duel with Theodora. Then the fool fell on his own sword in what I guess was some pointless gesture to prevent Theodora from breaking his mind and learning that he had sent his daughter and the medallion to Earth. Now it is your turn to die while I will live on forever, ruling both Janasara and Earth at the side of my empress."

Her grandfather and grandmother had sacrificed themselves to protect their daughter, Charlee's mom. But Tribon was wrong—their sacrifice had not been foolish. They had died bravely. Their deaths meant something. That thought rallied Charlee's strength. A wave of muscle-building energy rushed through her body. Tired eyes beamed and the pain from the gashes in her side eased.

"It's up to me now to finish what my grandparents started. I have to stop Theodora." But who was this Dragon Lord and why didn't he help? "Tribon, my grandfather was no fool. And I'm not going to go down without a fight."

"Good." Tribon gripped his sword with both hands.

Charlee backed into the outside wall of a prison house and braced herself against the rough, scratchy surface. The rotten scent of decay permeated the wall, or maybe the smell came from Tribon. The knight closed the gap, stopping just a sword's length away. The stench of rotten eggs poured from the wound inflicted by the bike.

Steady.

Tribon pointed the tip of his sword's blade at her stomach. In seconds he would strike to end her life. She had one chance to stop the giant if her strength lasted.

"Die, young knight!" Tribon whipped his sword in a circle, swinging toward her head.

Charlee dodged the blade as it whooshed over her head, slamming into the concrete with enough force to shake the wall. He hunched over and dropped the point of the blade to the ground. That gave Charlee just enough time. She dove under the giant knight's legs and then bounded up behind him. When Tribon turned, she smashed his jaw with both fists, toppling him onto his back. Unfortunately, he was still conscious. He moaned, rubbing his bearded chin but he would soon rise.

Breathing heavily, Charlee stared at Tribon waiting for him to rise—but it proved too long.

The air heated over her right shoulder. She raised her arms just in time to shield herself from a deadly discharge of the sorceress' magic. Her forearms took the blunt of the explosion but the force slammed her against the wall. Arms sizzling as the skin glowed red hot, Charlee slid to the ground. Her vision tunneled. She was slipping into unconsciousness. "Not yet. Can't… give…up. Stay alive," she mumbled. Placing her hands against the cement wall, Charlee slowly, painfully stood. She anticipated another attack by the sorceress, but the air around her had cooled—there was no sign of another energy assault. Theodora had no reason to deliver the final blow. Tribon could do that.

The knight planted his sword in front of her and leaned against it as he climbed to his feet. His face was contorted in pain and he spit out blood. Some stuck to his beard. "Brave, but meaningless. Now, taste steel."

There was nowhere to go…nowhere to escape. Leaning against the wall for support, Charlee gingerly touched her blistered forearms. She shuddered at the putrid odor of her own burnt skin. Whatever strength coursed through her body couldn't heal her fast enough—not without the bike.

With a laugh that echoed, Tribon swung his sword at her. With weak legs, Charlee crouched to her knees and covered her face.

CLING! CLANK! Steel smashed together. A sword blocked Tribon's blade. Peering up, she followed the crossed blades with her eyes, more surprised than she had ever been.

"Dad?"

Professor Smelton stood above her dressed in jeans and a white T-shirt with the words I *Love San Francisco* in black letters. The bandages were gone but his eyes were swollen and the skin purple underneath his wire-framed glasses.

His hands, steady and strong, wielded his weapon against Tribon's much larger blade.

"What? You thought we'd miss out on all the fun?" Her dad's voice shook with the effort, but he kept his sword pressed against Tribon's blade, blocking it. "What do you think I go to all those Renaissance faires for? Why do you think I practice sword fighting? I've been preparing for—"

Tribon kicked her dad in the chest. Their swords separated as her dad stumbled but he quickly regained his balance.

"All right, Tribon. We've never officially met—save for you attacking me in my office—but I know who and what you are." Charlee's dad sidestepped, his sword held like a baseball player awaiting that perfect pitch. "You betrayed my wife's father, and now you dare threaten my daughter. No more!"

Tribon sneered and waved her dad to attack. "What can a weak human hope to do against me?"

Charlee stared into her dad's bruised face. Though injured, he had come to rescue her. He was a warrior. "Dad don't. He's too strong. Get away from here. I'm so sorry for all the trouble I've caused you—sorry for trying to hurt you. Please, just go."

Her dad winked. "I'm the one who's sorry, but we'll have time for apologies later. Right now, I mean to make this overgrown snake pay for what he's done."

He leaped at Tribon, swinging his sword wildly. Tribon slashed back. Their steel collided and sparks flew. Then another familiar voice emerged.

"You are so right, Aunt Theodora. I should never have let my daughter stand in for me. Yet you know as well as I do it was her destiny. Admit you fear her power. That is why you wouldn't accept the medallion from her. Even if you had the medallion, she would still have the power to defeat you. She is the true heir to the Crown of Latara. Yet, though she has begun her journey bravely, it is time for me to continue the fight."

Charlee could not hold back tears. "Mom?"

Her mom nodded and offered the kind, all-knowing smile that said everything would be all right. She was dressed as Charlee had never seen, in a long black cloak that billowed around her body. Her long sandy hair was tied tightly into a ponytail, revealing light blue eyes that sparkled like a diamond. Her words—*destiny...power...heir...bravely begun her journey*—rang in Charlee's head.

"If it isn't my long-lost niece." Theodora placed her hands against her heart. "You don't know how long I have waited to be reunited with my family. You don't know how long I have waited to embrace you—embrace you until your energy bleeds out and is added to my power, just as I carry your mother's energy in me. I took it from her as I watched her die—well, as I killed her."

"Theodora, you didn't take all her energy," Charlee's mom approached the sorceress, seeming to float rather than walk. "My mother gave much of her strength to me. Tonight I will have revenge for her death."

"Ah! Such courageous words from such a frightened child." Theodora almost sang her response. "I await you."

Charlee's mom extended her right arm. A green ray exploded from her hand and raced toward Theodora. It slammed into the sorceress knocking her back. But she remained on her feet.

Wide-eyed, Charlee stared at her mom. Where had she gotten these powers? Why hadn't she ever told her about them? But her mom's powers were not enough. Theodora hadn't even attempted to block her mom's magic. The sorceress intended to weaken her mom in battle and then kill her. Charlee was not about to let that happen. She guessed her mom realized she was out-matched, but it wasn't going to stop her from putting up the best fight possible.

Charlee ran at Theodora but stopped when she heard her dad cry out. Tribon's sword had struck his arm. Her dad fought on, their swords crashing into each other in a dizzying display where the blades moved so fast, they seemed to vanish.

Her dad was hurt, and each blow further drained his strength. At last, he fell, knocked to the ground by a second kick from Tribon's massive boot.

Charlee dashed back toward her dad. She had to save him. Tribon stood ready to strike a final blow until a new voice caused the giant knight to back step with his eyes wide.

"Hold on, Tribon. Not so fast, old friend."

A puff of white smoke flashed next to Tribon and from it stepped the old pizza shop owner. He, too, held a sword.

"Cryton," Tribon choked. "You still live? Who else is going to be joining us tonight? Michala himself?"

"I am more alive than you, traitor." Mr. Levenstein, still dressed in greasy baking attire, lifted a sword. Where had he gotten that? Surely not hidden away in his pizza shop. "Now, why don't you bring that weapon my way? We have some unfinished business."

The two circled each other. Then Tribon lunged. Their swords clashed once, twice, three times. Charlee's dad joined the battle. How was it possible that old Mr. Levenstein—Cryton, as Tribon called him—was able to wield a sword this way? Who was this old man?

As the swordsmen fought, Theodora and Charlee's mom shot blasts of energy at each other. Theodora's bolts poured out in a stream of red, her mom's in flashing green. They lit up the island as if it was the Fourth of July.

Charlee's mom grew tired, her powers weakening. The bright green of her magic began to dim as Theodora advanced, the sorceress' magic clearly stronger than her mom's. And, while Mr. Levenstein and Charlee's dad fought well against Tribon, the knight infused with Theodora's twisted enchantment was more than they could handle.

Squeezing her eyes shut, Charlee held her head. They were losing the battle. All would soon be lost, unless…the medallion! She hadn't wanted to use it—wasn't even sure how to use it. But now she had no choice. It might be a first step toward the dark arts, but so be it.

Chapter 27

Thunder Rising

Light stabbed through the night. A sound roaring like approaching thunder stopped Charlee as she reached for the medallion. Overhead, the light separated into three. They had to be helicopters! Three of them, to be exact. And they approached fast.

A fourth helicopter appeared from the opposite direction, behind the island and hovered above Charlee's head. The wind from its swirling blades drove her to the ground. She sheltered her eyes from the dust storm. The helicopter seemed to hover forever. Then, as suddenly as it appeared, it vanished.

When she could see, four men stood over her—Deputy Chief Flores and three officers dressed in riot gear complete with helmets, shields, and rifles.

"Mr. Flores!" Charlee gasped.

"Did you think you could ditch me so easily?" A half-smile crossed the deputy chief's face.

The three other helicopters arrived at the island. Twelve more officers stood behind Mr. Flores. Off in the distance, a police boat raced toward Alcatraz.

"Sandra!" Mr. Flores ran toward his daughter as soon as he spotted her, but with a wave of her hand, Theodora cast an invisible barrier stopping him. He struck the wall with his shoulder over and over but could not break through. "Witch, give me back my daughter," he commanded.

Sandra knelt on the ground head bowed. At the sound of her dad's voice, she looked up and reached for him. Theodora drifted over to her and placed her hand on Sandra's head, stroking her hair.

"I see you have brought an army of warriors to face me, young coward." The sorceress glared at Charlee.

"I had nothing to do with it." Charlee positioned herself in front of Mr. Flores.

"This is a joyous night indeed," Theodora sang. "Now I can destroy them just as I destroyed Michala's army. I will have the satisfaction of taking everything from the Last Guardian—her family, her warriors and her friend."

"No, Theodora, let Sandra go." Charlee inched toward the sorceress.

Charlee's mom chimed in. "Theodora, this is between you and me now, no one else. Let that child go."

Once more, Theodora unleashed a curdling laugh. "Fools, I could squash you all, but I have a better plan. I think I will let you face my army of the good people of this world who have become my slaves. That way you have a choice—destroy them or be destroyed. I will watch and enjoy."

She chanted an incantation and a crowd of her mutated monsters gathered atop the roof of the prison house above them. They clawed at the night, crying out as their bodies writhed in agony. One command from Theodora and they would pounce, their human side unable to control the beasts they had become.

The officers responded, aiming their rifles.

Theodora kept laughing.

"I have to stop this," Charlee whispered. "Theodora wants blood. She can have mine."

Charlee marched toward the sorceress who still stood by Sandra. If the sorceress had erected any kind of magical barrier to protect herself, it didn't stop Charlee. "Enough. This ends now."

"What did you say?" Theodora's eyes blazed. "You are in no position to end anything. This amuses me and I will continue until I grow tired of it. Those who remain will bow to their empress or forfeit their lives."

"No, Theodora." Charlee stopped inches from Theodora. "This is what you wanted all along."

She held out the medallion and dropped to her knees. "Please, my empress. Take my soul, but leave the others unharmed. I promise to serve you faithfully if you'll just leave my friends, my family and my city alone. I will learn your ways. I now see your way is the only way."

Theodora laid a hand on Charlee's head. "Finally, you see that you cannot defeat me. That is why I allowed this battle to continue—so that you would come to understand the truth. Your mother is right. You have great power. I will teach you to use that power properly. You will stand by my side and help me to conquer all who come before me. Will you swear allegiance to me, guardian?"

"I will, but first take us away from here." Charlee grasped Theodora's hand. "I will do everything you say, but only when these people are safe."

"Child, no one will be safe from my power, but for now choose a site. But bear in mind, I want all to see you bow to me."

"There," Charlee said, pointing to the Golden Gate Bridge, which rose high above the Bay, an arching, massive superstructure that lighted up the night. "Take me there."

"Yes, that is a choice that pleases me." Theodora's eyes were wild. "From there my voice will fill this land and all who dwell here will know their true empress." Theodora embraced Charlee and the two became airborne.

"Charlee, no, don't do this." Her mom ran forward, but her husband and Mr. Levenstein stopped her.

Glancing back at her parents, Charlee nodded before she and Theodora floated away from the island. Once over the water they soared toward the bridge, a salty mist blowing across her face. The entire time, Charlee kept her eyes on her parents until the distance proved too great even for her stronger vision. As they disappeared from her view, Charlee fought back tears, knowing this was the end.

It only took seconds to reach the base of the bridge, but it felt like hours. From there, they ascended the peak of the south tower high above the bridge. The lights of the city across the Bay shimmered. *So peaceful*, she thought. By sacrificing herself, maybe things would stay that way.

Their ascension ended on a steel walkway high above the traffic. As her feet touched on the solid structure, Charlee peered down at the cars passing far underneath and at the water hundreds of feet below. She shivered against a strong, frigid wind. Did she have the nerve to do what she had to? Was she really prepared to die—at only thirteen? She wished she could go back to the life she had before this all started, but there was no going back. Apparently her life's course had been set.

Theodora was the first to speak. "Well, child, I have done as you have asked."

Charlee lowered to her knees and bowed her head. "Then I am ready to serve you."

"You lie!" Theodora's words were abrupt. She slapped Charlee in the face. It stung. "You think I cannot see into your soul. You think I cannot see that even now you plot against me. I have brought you to this splendid bridge because from here your family can watch you die. Your lifeless body will fall into the cold, dark waters." She took a breath. "Now death will come to you." An aura glowed around Theodora.

Charlee stood. "Theodora, you're right. I will die tonight, but not by your hands."

Still clutching the medallion, she dove off the south tower. Her body cleaved through the air as she plummeted to the abyss below.

She would either slam into the water and die—and the medallion would sink to the bottom with her—or if she truly was a guardian, *I can manage to open a gateway back to Theodora's world just before I hit the water. Then, if Theodora wants the medallion, she'll have to follow me back to her world.*

A third option presented itself. From where the sorceress stood on the south tower, she threw a magic lasso and snared Charlee. Tugging on the invisible rope, Theodora drew her back toward the tower.

"It's not that easy, child." Theodora's voice boomed over the Bay.

Charlee fought to break free, but that only tightened the rope's grip. No, she had to break free. Charlee reached out with her mind. *Bike, if you're out there, I need your strength!* As the sorceress hoisted her back to the bridge, Charlee's arms and legs began to tingle. The sensation filled her chest. Heart pounding stronger, blood moving faster, her face felt hot and her body trembled. Whether fueled by rage or by the bike—or by some other force—an untapped power coursed through her.

Gripping the medallion with one hand, she grabbed Theodora's magic rope with the other and heaved with all her new strength. Theodora stumbled and struggled to keep her footing.

Again the sorceress' voice sounded over the Bay. "What are you doing?"

Charlee jerked the rope again, and Theodora almost fell. This time, however, the sorceress tightened the magic, squeezing so that that it tore through flesh.

"One more time," Charlee wailed. Closing her eyes, willing power into her hand, she yanked even harder.

Theodora fell from the tower.

Her scream cracked as loud as lightning. Charlee then flung the medallion toward the sea, just the way she would toss a Frisbee. Theodora's anguished cry ripped across the Bay as the medallion fell toward the water below. Angling her body, Theodora dove past Charlee, reaching the medallion before it hit the water. Charlee fell, too, as the sorceress' magical lasso somehow still attached dragged her toward the sea.

Now! Summoning whatever power she had, Charlee pictured the creek where she had first seen Theodora. Holding the image clear in her mind, she opened a gateway directly beneath the sorceress. The gateway formed as a tiny blue ball which grew into a tear of light just above the sea. Below them, the tear expanded into a portal large enough for Theodora.

"What have you—"

The sorceress' cry was cut short as she, with the medallion clutched in her hand, slipped through the gateway. Charlee was going to follow into the blue light unless she could force the portal closed. *Come on!* She unleashed her last bit of strength, the pressure in her head like a vice grip crushing her skull—but it worked. The gateway closed seconds before she fell through.

Now, the sea rushed toward her, wind stinging her face. Still she smiled. Theodora was gone as if she had never crossed the gateway in the first place—as if it all had been a dream.

Charlee had done what needed to be done. Comforting warmth cocooned her body. Then darkness hit.

Chapter 28

A Father's Hand

Charlee was sure she was dead—swallowed by the water, just as the bike had been. Somehow, she was still wrapped in the comforting warmth that had surrounded her before she hit the water. If this was what death was like, it wasn't so bad.

A hand, then two hands, grabbed her body and lifted her. Then came a voice...a good voice. "Baby girl, I've got you." It sounded like...Dad? "Hang in there. You're safe."

Charlee opened her eyes and stared into her dad's face. Over his head the sky rushed by. She was in her dad's arms and her mom, Mr. Flores, and Sandra were also there. Sandra! She was all right...unless Charlee was dead and imagining this.

Sandra smiled and looked so alive. Frozen tears streaked her cheeks but her eyes were strong and clear. Her friend had returned.

"Dad," Charlee whispered.

Both her parents had misty eyes. "You're all right," her dad repeated. "You're safe. We're in the police boat heading back to shore."

"What happened?" Charlee asked.

"You did it," he answered. "You saved us all."

"But what happened to Tribon? What happened to the people Theodora changed?"

Her dad laughed. "I told you she couldn't just rest. As soon as you sent Theodora back to her world, Tribon faded away too."

"Of course, Theodora held Tribon's heart," Charlee said, wearily and still disoriented. "Where ever Theodora is, Tribon has to follow. That is how she brought him across the gateway in the first place. He had to return back to their world with her."

That was his curse.

Charlee flinched as her mom placed a hand on her shoulder. A searing heat flowed from the touch.

"Try not to move," her mom urged. "You have bad burns and that gash at your side. This heat you feel is going to help."

Charlee glanced one more time at Sandra, who sat close wrapped in a blanket with her dad's arm around her. Standing over them all was the old pizza shop owner. A sword hung at his side. He nodded to her and smiled. Who was this man? She held that question as another thought filled her mind.

"And the people?" she asked again. "All those poor people Theodora changed?"

"They're fine. Theodora's spell is broken. The police are tending to them," her dad explained.

Charlee tilted her head back. She stopped Theodora in time. All the people Theodora had changed would return to their human form as the sorceress was now a dimension away—her magic broken before it could become permanent.

"You did well, honey." Charlee's dad grasped her hand. "I am proud of you."

"And Megan? Where is my sister?"

"Don't worry. All is well."

"Dad…"

"Enough, now. We're taking you to the hospital. There will be time for talking later."

"And time for planning," Charlee's mom kept her hand pressed against Charlee's shoulder, but the painful heat had eased.

"What do you mean?" Charlee grabbed her mom's arm.

Her mom gave her a loving smile. "Tonight was an important victory. You met your destiny bravely and with honor. But now I must show the same courage. I must return home. Theodora has the medallion, and her power will only increase as she becomes immortal. She may have conquered the Ten Unified Kingdoms of Janasara long ago, but after tonight's defeat she will seek further vengeance against the people there. I cannot sit by any longer."

She frowned as she looked over Charlee's wounds. "But we must tend to your injuries before you go into shock. I…I am so sorry I allowed this to happen to you, but your destiny required…"

Her words gave way to sobs. Charlee reached up and gave her mom a long hug. "Mom, I have to show you something."

"What?"

"Lift the back of my shirt."

Charlee's mom did as asked, revealing a length of wide tape that encircled Charlee's waist. Under the tape was the medallion.

"What…?"

"It was her idea," Mr. Flores quipped.

"But how…?" Charlee's mom asked.

Charlee smiled weakly. "A mini-Frisbee and some black paint, Mom."

"It was brilliant in its simplicity," Mr. Flores added. "Really, your daughter came up with it on her own."

"Well, sort of." Charlee's eyes sought out Mr. Flores. "When you threw the medallion to me at the museum, you gave me the idea."

"I don't understand," Charlee's mom said.

"I painted a mini-Frisbee with black paint and hung it around my neck, like it was the real medallion." Charlee stopped to catch her breath. Exhaustion was starting to overtake her. "I just hoped that at one point in the battle, I would have the chance to open a gateway and throw it in so that Theodora would follow it, thinking it the real medallion."

"How did you know you'd get the chance to trick her?" her dad asked.

Charlee closed her eyes momentarily. "I didn't. If she didn't fall for it, the only other thing I could do is open a gateway to somewhere for myself and the real medallion and hope she would come after me."

"So when you jumped, you were truly prepared to sacrifice yourself." Mr. Flores held his daughter's head to his chest and stroked her hair.

Charlee reached for both her mom and dad's hand. "Yes."

Chapter 29

Healing Powers

"The pace of your recovery is remarkable, young lady," said Dr. Lorenzo, checking beneath the bandages that covered the burns on Charlee's hands and arms. The doctor also scanned the half a dozen other injuries, including slash marks on her side and bite marks on her shoulder. "It's only been two days since you were admitted, but it looks like you have been recovering for weeks, maybe longer."

The doctor paused.

There was much he didn't know about his young patient. He just knew from the Police Department that she had been hurt while in the service of the police and that her case was not to be spoken of with any unnecessary personnel or anyone outside the hospital.

"This is one for the medical journals." The doctor flipped through Charlee's medical chart then tore it up. "Too bad it will never be documented. Well, I'll be back to check on you in a few hours."

"Thanks, doc," Charlee said from her hospital bed where she lay restlessly. She wished she could just walk out and get back to her life…whatever that meant these days. But she couldn't just leave. Mr. Flores had stationed officers outside the hospital room. Sandra's dad had said it was just a precautionary step for her protection, but she figured it was to make sure she stayed in the hospital for as long as the doctors felt it necessary.

When Dr. Lorenzo left the room, Charlee turned to her mom, whose healing magic was the real reason she was recovering so fast.

Charlee found out that when she hit the water after jumping from the bridge it had been her mom's magic she felt. That's why she survived. Her mom had reached out and surrounded her in a protective bubble just as she struck the water.

"Ready, Charlee," her mom said, stepping forward.

"Yeah." She really wasn't. Her mom's healing touch actually kind of stung.

Her mom placed her hands on Charlee's arms, closed her eyes, and uttered an incantation. Charlee grimaced. Her arms tingled. That sensation quickly grew in intensity until she wanted to break free from her mom's touch. But just as quickly as it began, the sensation softened to soothing warmth.

"Soon, you'll be well enough to leave here." Her mom leaned against a chair, drained from the effort.

"I'm well enough now."

"No, honey," said her dad, who held Megan in his arms. Charlee's sister slept, breathing peacefully "Give it just a bit more time."

Fidgeting in her bed, Charlee searched for a comfortable position despite the bandages which limited movement. Aggravated, she gave up trying and focused her attention on her parents.

"Mom, Dad, I have so many questions."

Her mom was the first to speak. "We can find the answers together when you are better."

"No, I need some answers now."

Her parents exchanged glances. "Perhaps you're right, Charlee. We've put this off long enough," her dad lamented. He eyed Megan to ensure she was still asleep and glanced at the door as if checking that it was closed. It was. "Go ahead and ask your questions."

Charlee sighed. "Who am I?"

Her mom sat at the bedside and caressed Charlee's cheek. She had shadows under her eyes and a furrowed brow but her smile was calming. "You are the person you have always been—Charleya Smelton, our daughter. But you are also a young girl of great power whose blood comes partly from another world called Janasara. You are a guardian, as your grandfather, my father, Michala. As a guardian, the first female guardian that I know of, you have an ability I could never understand, an ability to open a gateway, apparently one that can connect worlds."

Taking hold of Charlee's hand, her mom gently squeezed before continuing to speak. "But there's more. You also have the blood of your grandmother, Queen Assara, who ruled the Kingdom of Latara and led the Council of the Ten Unified Kingdoms. She was a powerful conjurer. I have some of her power and you have some of my power, which you have only begun to understand. Each conjurer's ability manifests itself differently. Each wielder must discover their power and learn to use it."

Her mom leaned in closer. "You must also understand that as my first-born daughter, you are heir to the Crown of Latara. It may very well be your destiny to wear the crown and lead a new Council."

Charlee pondered her mom's words for a moment. This was all so much to understand. Now she was supposed to be the heir to some kingdom in another world. What if she didn't want any of this? What if she wanted to be the same nerdy teen she was before the dreams began?

"I don't want to be...queen," she said, her voice revealing a spark of anger.

"I understand." Her mom nodded. "And I—we—will make sure you have that choice." She rose and walked over to her husband, who sat in a chair rocking Megan. She placed a hand on his shoulder.

"You know, I have a lot to figure out, but I think I know one thing." Charlee blinked away the sleepiness threatening to overtake her. "I think it's my magic—I know what my ability is. I figured it out when I was able to use Theodora's own magic and knock her off the bridge."

"And what is it?" her mom asked.

"I think I can draw energy from others, and I can use that energy to gain...powers. That's why when I touched the bike its energy gave me strength. I could hear and see things better, too, you know, like superpowers."

Her mom smiled and returned to her bedside. "I'm proud of you, Charlee. You have begun your journey toward becoming perhaps the greatest guardian infused with two very special powers. You may choose not to be queen, but you cannot escape your destiny as a guardian. That's why we couldn't tell you about your true family history or warn you of the danger you might face in your life. The Ancient Scrolls of the Unified Kingdoms tell that the Last Guardian must alone discover what it is to be a guardian."

"Am I truly the Last Guardian?" Charlee asked.

"Time will tell," her mom answered.

That response made Charlee gulp loudly. She didn't want to be. To think that there were none like her...no one to teach her...no one who could fully understand her, not ever her mom, made her feel alone. Her stomach suddenly felt empty, her chest heavy.

It also reminded her that she was the only one who could open a portal to Janasara where Theodora was trapped. If that were the case, would the sorceress again haunt her dreams? So far Theodora hadn't, but it was only a matter of time before she resurfaced.

Fear crept over Charlee and she started to sweat.

She tried to force that thought from her mind and again concentrate on her parents. She still had so many other questions. "So why did you come to rescue me if I was to face evil on my own?"

"You're our daughter," her dad replied, his voice grave. "We figured... well...to heck with the Scrolls."

157

Another question crossed her mind. "How did you guys and Mr. Levenstein even get to the island? I don't remember a boat other than the police boat, which came after you were already there."

Her mom answered. "I have limited levitation magic. I hadn't used it, I guess, since you were born. I wasn't sure it would work, but it got us there. It did weaken me though. I think your father has put on a few extra pounds. That and I'm really out of practice."

"I resent that weight crack," her dad joked. "Don't let your mother fool you. She is a powerful conjurer. Why she ever married an average guy like me I'll never know."

Her parents hugged carefully so as not to wake Megan.

Charlee considered what her dad said. He was not from that world called Janasara. He was just a nice guy from Earth who had met and fallen in love with a woman in college who was just a little different than other women.

He had married that woman and sworn to protect her, even going so far as to become an expert swordsman to defend her and their family should the day come when a threat would rise.

My dad is a good man, Charlee realized as she slowly let sleep overcome her. *I'll have to let him know that. It's long overdue.*

Chapter 30

Getting To Know Cryton

"How does it feel to be out of the hospital?" asked the old man Charlee had just days ago known as Mr. Levenstein.

"I'm still sore, but I feel a lot better," she said to the man she now knew as Cryton.

Charlee gazed into Cryton's blue eyes as he spoke. Whereas once they had looked tired, now they were sharp. Even his limp was gone. He now walked straight up and strong as he delivered her a slice of cheese pizza at his deli and pizza shop.

It had all been an act—part of his disguise. "I sure am proud of the young girl...young woman...you have become." Cryton sat in the booth next to her. "I have watched you your whole life, and I knew you had a guardian in your heart."

"Why, Cryton...why have you stayed away?" she asked, blowing on her pizza. "Even if you didn't want me to know your real identity, you could have...I don't know...pretended to be my grandfather."

Cryton nodded and smiled softly. "A long time ago, your mother, father and I decided it would be best if I remain in the shadows so to speak. That gave me the freedom to watch over your family from afar, and if the time ever came, I could provide an element of surprise against any threat. Of course, in the meantime," he chuckled, "I became an old man."

"And was it you who somehow made me decide to leave the bike in the alley next to your shop?" she queried, taking her first bite of pizza. "I mean how could that have just happened?"

"I've thought long and hard about that, actually," Cryton offered. "And while I had nothing to do with it, I do think somehow you were drawn here as we were destined to meet."

Charlee took another bite of pizza. She had no choice but to accept that answer. She had learned while in the hospital that her mom, her injured dad, and little sister had gone to Cryton's pizza shop after leaving the hospital. The pizza shop also served as a place to hide Megan. She had slept under the watchful eyes of Cryton's—or rather Mr. Levenstein's—baker as the battle on Alcatraz took place. That baker, an old gentleman who had worked for Mr. Levenstein for years, knew nothing of Cryton's true identity. The baker only understood that he was to babysit Megan that night.

Charlee also discovered it was her mom's voice she heard in her head, telling her to remain calm at times when she thought all was lost. Her mom had used her magic to keep a mental lock on Charlee at all times. She was never truly alone.

Cryton took a bite of pizza himself. "Charlee, what you did to that vile beast, Theodora, would have made your grandfather so proud."

"But, Cryton, I let her live, and now she's back in Janasara and the people there are probably worse off."

"Probably."

"I have to do something."

"You have done your part. It's now time for others to continue this effort to stop Theodora."

Cryton spoke about himself, her mom, and dad. They wanted her to open a gateway as soon as she was fully healed and could care for her little sister, with the help of her dad's extended Smelton family. But she didn't agree. It was her responsibility to face Theodora again.

Charlee changed the subject. "Cryton, tell me again about how you came to Earth."

Cryton eased back in the booth. "Your grandfather was my closest friend. When he told me he had a special mission, one that would send me through a gateway to another world, I didn't know what to think. When he told me I would be entrusted with his daughter, your mother, I said no. I wanted to stay and fight. But he made me promise that should he fall in battle, should I never hear from him again, that I was to raise his daughter as my own in this world."

Cryton took a deep breath. "That's what I tried to do to the best of my ability. I raised her and taught her of her true identity. I shared the teachings of our people and of the Ancient Scrolls of the Unified Kingdoms, which told of a Last Guardian. Yes, I did the best I could to raise her and teach her along with watching over the medallion until I passed it on to your mother and your father."

Charlee listened intently. "Cryton, am I really the Last Guardian?"

"You are a guardian. Are you the Last Guardian foretold of in the Scrolls? You may very well be. Certainly, your mother, though powerful in her magic, did not receive the guardian abilities, but that is not the first time that power skipped a generation. And the Scrolls are not specific about whether the Last Guardian would be male or female."

Cryton paused for a moment as if gathering his next thought. "Whether you are the last or not doesn't really matter, does it? All that matters is that you have brought hope. As word of you reaches the Unified Kingdoms and all of Janasara that may be enough of a spark to kindle a revolution and topple Theodora."

All the more reason she had to go there. "Cryton, I can accept being some guardian, but I don't want to be a queen. Let my mom be queen and Megan after her."

Cryton was silent for several moments. "You must do what you think is best, but don't be afraid to be who you are. It is a gift."

Charlee lowered her pizza and leaned toward Cryton. "Can you tell me about the Dragon Lord? Tribon said the Dragon Lord chose not to help my grandfather, why?"

"The Dragon Lord was a coward," the old man shifted in his seat. "The dragons and the Ten Unified Kingdoms lived in peace and I thought we were allies, but when Theodora rose to power, their leader, the Dragon Lord, stood by while our people fought and died. I do not know why, but if I ever return to Janasara, I will first kill Theodora then the Dragon Lord. I do not wish to discuss it further."

Charlee breathed deeply. She would accept that answer for now. Then her thoughts turned toward her fallen protector—the bike. "Can you tell me more about my bike?"

"I have to be honest, until the events of the last week occurred, I knew nothing of the bike," Cryton said. "All I knew when I came across the gateway is that Michala had also sent a magical being with great power to this world as a secret protector to watch over your mother and one day to watch over her children."

"And you never knew what it was or where it was?"

"I always had the feeling I was being watched, but I accepted it," Cryton explained. "I now know the being was a Changeling—a creature I thought was merely legend even for Janasara. Changelings are said to be beings of pure energy. That's why you gained so much strength and power from it. Its energy helped you discover your own...abilities. But the Changeling had its role to play just as I had mine. It knew at some point it might have to sacrifice itself as I was prepared to sacrifice myself. Your...bike...was very brave."

"But how did the Changeling know I needed him now?"

"Changelings are strange creatures. They are said to have abilities I could never understand." Cryton gazed up as if looking toward the Bay, where the bike—the Changeling—perished. "He must have sensed the danger coming."

Charlee lowered her head. Tears formed. She chuckled as she wiped the tears away. "Yeah, well, he might have been able to sense danger, but he didn't have much sense of cool."

Cryton looked puzzled. "What do you mean?"

Charlee rubbed her eyes. "If he was this Changeling that could take any form, why not take the form of a dirt bike, maybe even a mountain bike— why not a motorcycle."

"I think I know why he took the form of that old bike," Cryton answered. "You yourself have told me that he took the form of a dove in the museum. I bet he also took the form of a dove to watch over you at your home. That means he probably had a pretty good view of your father's den through a window. Your mother reminded me of this just the other day. In the den is a picture of your father when he was a child with a white bike identical to the one the Changeling became."

"He must have saw that picture and…well, it was still a bad choice." Charlee lowered her head. Even though the bike had been part of her life for a short time, it felt as if she had lost a brother or a sister. She should have been able to save the bike just as the bike had saved her, but she failed. Charlee would never forgive herself for that.

"Charlee, this won't make you feel any better, but I have a gift for you. Wait here." Cryton rose from the booth and disappeared to the back room of his pizza shop. In the time he was gone, Charlee could not erase the image of Tribon's sword driven through the bike in its unicorn form.

"I'm so sorry, bike," she whispered, striking the table with a fist. "I promise I won't stop until Theodora is dead."

When Cryton reappeared he held something wrapped in cloth. "It would mean the world to me if you would accept this gift."

"What is it?" she asked.

Cryton un-wrapped the cloth and held before him a long-bladed sword, its steel shimmering in the lights of the pizza shop. The handle was silver, but it was simple and unadorned.

"This was my sword when I fought alongside your grandfather in defending the Unified Kingdoms," Cryton said, caressing the blade. "It served me well, and now I think it is time for a new owner to wield it."

"Cryton, no."

162

"You dare say no to me?"

Charlee shook her head and reached for the sword. It was heavy, but it felt good in her hands. "I'll accept this on one condition."

Cryton raised an eyebrow. "And that is?"

"That you teach me to use it."

He laughed. "Well, now…let's begin."

Chapter 31

Theodora's Revenge

She was dreaming once again.

It had to be a dream because just moments ago, she slept safely in bed, lying with Cryton's sword at her side. Now, she stood in what looked like a castle throne room, one with a balcony that looked over a kingdom. With cautious steps, she strolled out onto the observation deck. The view sickened her.

It seemed to be the realm she had seen before when she first allowed Theodora to cross through the gateway. Only now all the nature that had made it seem so alive was gone. The land stood in ruins. Factories spewed thick columns of black smoke which rose toward a gray sky.

"Welcome, Guardian."

Charlee quickly spun around at the sound of Theodora's voice. "Get out of my head, Theodora."

"Never."

Her great-aunt had once again taken on the form of a beautiful princess. "I'm not going to open a gateway for you, Theodora. That's not going to happen. I am stronger now. If we are going to meet in dreams, I can control it."

"My dear girl, I have no wish for you to open a gateway for me." Theodora floated onto a railing near where Charlee stood. "No, I have only sought you out to invite you to your true home. I want you to come to me and bring me what is rightfully mine and I know you will."

"Why is that?" Charlee was wary of Theodora but also watched out for Tribon.

"For one, I think you wish to unlock the secrets of the medallion. I know you saw your face in the medallion. I know you question what that means."

How did she know that? Charlee tried to control her emotions. "I don't know what you're talking about."

"Don't you? Even now don't you feel the medallion calling to you? Don't you crave its power?"

Charlee swallowed. Theodora was right. Since she was released from the hospital she had spent sleepless nights staring at a safe where her dad kept the medallion. She longed to open it and touch it. Just being close to the safe made her face turn red, her hands clammy. She often heard the medallion calling out to her, urging her to use its power, or maybe she was just going crazy. It took all her strength not to take it. It got tougher every day to keep her distance, though eventually she would have to use it against Theodora.

"I'm not like you, Theodora," Charlee said meekly.

"I can see you lie, young guardian," Theodora approached Charlee, circling her. "I can help you find the answers. All you need to do is bring me my medallion. You can even be queen, answering only to me, your empress."

Charlee backed away. "That's not going to happen."

Theodora vanished, but her voice remained. "I thought you might say that, so I have something else that should cause you to change your mind."

In a heartbeat, Theodora reappeared and this time she was not alone. Standing with her, with chains around its wings and long neck was a bird creature Charlee recognized from one of her early dreams.

"Saur!" Charlee nearly shouted to the bird that looked like a small giraffe.

The half bird half giraffe creature spoke in its own strange language. "It is good to see you again, although I wish it could be under different circumstances. Do not do what this sorceress asks of you, no matter what she does to me."

"Quiet," Theodora commanded.

"Saur, I'll get you out of this!" Charlee stepped toward the bird.

Theodora laughed. "I warned you guardian that others would pay for your insolence and now you can see for yourself what that means."

"Theodora, no," Charlee begged.

"It seems our friend here has a bit of magic in him, and since I rule this world, that magic belongs to me, so I think I will take it…now."

"Saur, hold on!" Charlee rushed toward the bird only to be forced back by a wave of Theodora's hand, knocking her down.

The sorceress embraced the winged creature. A crimson glow radiated from her body and encircled the bird. Saur began to shake and gasped quiet screams.

Charlee, held down by Theodora's magical grip, thrashed around the floor. She couldn't reach Saur. She locked eyes with the bird and saw the creature's agony. If this were a dream, she could do whatever she wanted. Charlee could save him.

She ripped free of Theodora's hold and jumped at the sorceress only to watch her vanish again. Charlee landed on the deck and turned to see Saur, his body withered to little more than bones. He was dead.

Charlee held the bird in her arms. She quivered with rage. "Have it your way, Theodora! You want me here…I'll be here."

Theodora never reappeared but her words filled Charlee's head. "I await you, guardian."

§ § §

Charlee awoke to find herself clutching her pillow. Fresh tears filled her eyes. Had she really just witnessed Saur die at the hands of Theodora, or was it truly nothing more than a dream…a nightmare. Either way, she had to face Theodora.

Checking her clock, she saw it was 6 a.m., and she could no longer sleep. She opened the bedroom window of the beachfront home her parents had rented while their house was being repaired. A cool damp mist hovered over the neighborhood.

In a few hours, she would go see Sandra. In the past two weeks since the night on Alcatraz, they had short chaperoned visits by their parents who worried they both still needed time to heal. Maybe they worried she and Sandra would find some new mischief if left alone. Today, though, would be their first time alone together, and they were going to M's for burgers, soda, and video games.

Charlee couldn't wait to see her friend, but she was restless now. She decided to take a ride and think about all that had occurred. She made her way to the nearby pier on a red beach cruiser, a gift from the Police Department. The spreading sunlight broke through the mist by the time she reached the pier, still deserted save a few harbor workers.

As the ocean view cleared, she stared across the Bay toward Alcatraz. It seemed like such a long time ago that she battled Theodora.

Charlee gazed skyward as a group of seagulls flew by. She decided to test her powers. Reaching out to the birds with her mind, she attempted to tap into their life energy. They were small winged creatures and didn't have much to offer, but her mind suddenly felt free of burdens, like she was flying among the seagulls. The energy she consumed from the birds strengthened her vision enough to remove her glasses and enhanced her hearing. That power though was nothing like what she felt when in contact with that strange shape-shifting creature that had given its life for hers.

With the help of Mr. Flores and the Police Department, she had scoured the Bay for the bike—or any strange out-of-the-ordinary creature that might be the Changeling—but nothing had been found. The bike, her protector, was truly gone.

"I miss you so much," she said, placing her glasses back on as the birds' energy quickly slipped away.

Just then the pier shook as a thunderous rumbling rose from the sea and rocked the wooden pylons. She grabbed a railing and glanced toward the water. Rolling waves splashed beneath her. Then, the quiet returned. It must have been a small California earthquake.

As she released the railing, another trembler struck, this time stronger than the first. It knocked her to the ground and threw white seawater foam into the air.

"What's happening?"

The pier swayed from side to side, preventing Charlee from standing. Waves crashed harder. Then a streak of light shot up from the sea and rose into the sky. A wall of water swelled over where she stood. Charlee ducked her head but the seawater was blinding. Blinking, she pushed her glasses up on her nose as she struggled to regain her vision.

What was that? She got to her feet and stopped…and gasped. "Bike!"

Charlee took off her glasses to rub her eyes. Could it be? Were her eyes playing tricks on her?

It certainly looked like the bike—the same old junky-looking heap of metal with the banana seat and rusted white paint. It stood on the pier next to the much-fancier beach cruiser.

"Bike, is it you?" Charlee tried to hold back the tears. In response, the bike spread its wings and knocked over the cruiser. It rolled forward until it stood right in front of her. Was this a Theodora trick? "Bike, I watched you…die."

The bike moved its handlebars and right front tire as if to shake its head… as if to say, "Not quite." It then transformed…first into a white dove…then into a unicorn, and finally into a glob of yellow glowing orb that hovered in front of her. It looked like a large single-cell organism, like those she saw through a microscope in science class.

The glob approached her. Charlee stepped back. It then formed a glowing hand that reached out for her. Charlee hesitated. The glowing hand extended farther, bridging the distance.

"Bike, what are you doing?" In the next moment, the glowing fingers touched her hand. Energy rushed through her, like she had felt before when in contact with the bike. The connection provided answers.

Images raced through her mind. Of her grandfather, the Guardian Michala. Of a young Changeling asked to make a sacrifice…to leave the world it had known to watch over the guardian's child. Of Charlee's own birth as seen by a white dove sitting on a windowsill outside a hospital. A sense of awe for this mysterious creature washed over her.

She knew then. "You are…my bike." The Changeling released its grip then transformed back into the bike with wings. "Thank you for coming back to me." Charlee smiled wide. "I promise to do all I can to protect you, just as you have protected me."

She climbed onto the bike and removed her glasses.

"You know, I'm not really sure what to call you. You don't have a name. I know you're not really a bike. But if you don't mind, I'd still like to call you…bike."

The bike responded with a thrust of its powerful wings.

"Yeah!" Charlee shouted as they launched skyward. Her companion was back. Now she knew she could do what she had to. She could face Theodora again—soon.

But that could wait—at least for the moment. Now, she just wanted to do a little flying with the greatest bike anyone could ever have.

Acknowledgements

I would like to thank the team at Divertir Publishing, especially Kenneth Tupper and Jen Corkill, for their efforts in helping to edit my novel and in preparing the book for publication. I also thank those friendly readers who helped me through the writing process. Finally, I wish to acknowledge the editing support I received from Jill Ronsley early in the creation of this book.